Spd D8n

By Martin Lindsay

Moody Lapcat Books

First paperback edition in 2022

Design and Cover by Martin Lindsay

Images by Martin Lindsay and DAPA Images/Canva.

ISBN: 978-0-6451987-0-6 (paperback)

ISBN: 978-0-6451987-1-3 (ebook)

Published by Moody Lapcat Books

Perth, Western Australia

www.moodylapcatbooks.com

contact@moodylapcatbooks.com

Performing rights

Any performance or public reading of Spd D8n is forbidden unless a licence has been received from the author or the author's agent. The purchase of this book in no way gives the purchaser the right to perform the play in public, whether by the means of a staged production or a reading

All applications for public performance should be directed to the playwright c/- Moody Lapcat Books.

www.moodylapcatbooks.com

contact@moodylapcatbooks.com

Copying for educational purposes

The Australian Copyright Act 1968 (Act) allows a maximum of one chapter or 10% of this book, whichever is the greater, to be reproduced and/or communicated by any educational institution for its educational purposes provided that educational institution or the body that administers it) has given a remuneration notice to Copyright Agency Limited (CAL) under the Act.

For details of the CAL license for educational institutions contact CAL, Tel: (02) 9394 7600; email: info@copyright.com.au.

Copying for other purposes

Except as permitted under the Act, for example a fair dealing for the purposes of study, research, criticism or review, all

Contents

Characters

MIKE – 20's/30's

"No, I guess it doesn't get better with practice."

What he lacks in self-confidence Mike makes up for with the optimism that patiently following the rules of love will eventually find his match.

JACQUI – 20's/30's

"Yes, I do know how to have fun, thank you very much."

Known as "The Robot" at school, Jacqui is a strait-laced young woman unafraid to speak her mind with little tolerance for riff raff.

TOM – 20's/30's

"I don't want to be here anyway."

Jaded from a break-up, Tom is a sarcastic young man who just wants to be somewhere else.

CHLOE – 20s/30s

"Oh god, I've become the Personality Girl, haven't I?"

Beneath Chloe's bubbly demeanour hides a quiet desperation that she will never make anyone's grade.

JOANNE – early 40's

"What happened to my demographic?"

No one warned Joanne that 40 is not actually the new 30, and she is determined to get her money's worth of reclaimed youth no matter who stands in her way.

BOUNCER – any age – Non-Speaking

A suitably burly person of stern demeanour, capable of moving furniture and props while patrolling with an eagle eye.

Drunk NUDE GUY – any age

In the absence of a cameo by the writer, any available and daring crew member/front-of-house staff will suffice.

Setting

A pub function room, largely bare.

Across the front of stage are five TABLES, with CHAIRS, spot-lit independently. Entrances from either side which lead off to other unseen parts of the function room.

Characters will bring on personal props as they sit/depart. The tables should have compartments for various pre-loaded props that are "exchanged" during scenes.

Production Notes

- The cast largely deliver their lines to a fourth wall "Opposite" at the other side of their tables. Directions for these imaginary characters are sometimes specified in order to aid the cast's eye-lines and reactions.

- The performers will regularly "listen" to their "Opposite" replying (indicated by a new line starting with an ellipsis) but should always be mindful of pacing.

- It is up to the director and the performance space whether the TABLES and CHAIRS should be set and remain on stage for the entire performance. If preferred, or space is limited, the BOUNCER (and other similarly clad stage crew) can be utilised to bring furniture on and off "in-character".

- It is suggested the tables have a raised "lip" so that props can be placed out of sight. For example, in scenes with two characters passing objects to each other, to give the illusion that they are at opposite ends of the same table.

First Performed

Blak Yak Theatre, August 2017

Directed by Therese Cruise

Original Cast

Mike – Jonathan Cooper

Jacqui – Susan Veart

Tom – Stuart Porter

Chloe – Imogen Blackwell

Joanne – Melissa Merchant

Bouncer – Anthony O'Brien

Nude Guy – Martin Lindsay

ACT ONE

Scene 1.1 – Meet Mike

SOUND FX: Bell tinkle.

LIGHTS up.

MIKE sits nervously at TABLE with PINT glass.

MIKE

Hello! Well, here we are. I'm Michael.

MIKE offers hand to shake, withdraws when no hand is forthcoming, then quickly shakes when his "Opposite" offers hand after all.

MIKE

Yeah, I was dragged in by friends too.
Not that I'm saying it's Village of the Damned in here or anything. *(Points)* I mean, that girl over there is *gorgeous*. If someone like her is speed dating, then there's hope for the rest of us.
… Are you okay?
Anyway, our time is ticking. You start.

MIKE listens, nodding eagerly.

MIKE

Cool. That must be really cool.
… Well, it sounds sort of cool.

Me? Oh. Well, I work most of the week, *(Finger quotes)* "for da man". *(Instantly regrets).* I spend most of my spare time with friends doing … stuff. Oh! And I watch tv.
But mostly I go out. Most of the time. Mostly meeting people. Mostly. Not "The One" as yet obviously. How about you? Meaning *what do you do*, not "Are you The One". Not jumping to conclusions or anything. Though you seem nice, so that's a good first step on the road to "One-ness". But you know, baby steps.
Not that I'm saying I'm after kids straight away. Shit no. But obviously I'm open to having kids. At some stage.
Not tonight certainly.

MIKE takes a nervous drink.

MIKE

Surprising how long four minutes is, isn't it? Last speed dating I went to was ridiculously quick. Barely time to think, so we all just blathered nonsense.
… How do you mean, what's my excuse this time?
Anyway, this one is a lot more relaxed.

MIKE takes another nervous drink.

MIKE

So that's quite a bit we have in common already. You and me. With our working, doing stuff, and catching up with friends.

MIKE gives a polite laugh then instantly self-conscious.

MIKE

No, speed dating's normally like this.
… No, I guess it doesn't get better with practice.
(Sudden thought) Oh! I like your … how you've
done your hair. It's really … nice.

SOUND FX: Bell tinkle.

*MIKE makes a conspicuous tick on his score CARD, then beams a
smile.*

LIGHTS down.

Scene 1.2 – Meet Jacqui

SOUND FX: Bell tinkle.

LIGHTS up.

*JACQUI sits at a different TABLE with a score CARD, a GLASS
of water, and NOTEPAD.*

JACQUI

Hello. I'm Jacqui.

JACQUI points at NAMETAG then watches "Opposite" write.

JACQUI

… One C.

She nods approval at "Opposite's" spelling correction.

JACQUI

And you are? *(Writes)* And that's with an A or an E?

… Well, it's either one or the other.

… An A. Thank you.

She documents the time from her WATCH then lifts NOTEPAD.

JACQUI

Now, rather than aimless chit chat, I've prepared a few fun questions to keep things moving along.

… I said they were fun, didn't I?

(Reads) What's your favourite thing about your occupation?

…*(Frowns)* What is your occupation?

… How did you get into that line of work? Did you not study or something?

(Shakes head) Question two. If you were a stalker, which window of my house would you try to look in?

… I'm not accusing you. It's just a fun question revealing something about your personality. You seem very defensive about this.

… Well, yes, I suppose if I lived on a fourth floor, any window would be an abseiling feat effort worthy of congratulation. That's not the point.

I'll put you down as a bathroom window.

JACQUI writes but is interrupted.

JACQUI

(Frowns) About fifteen in total.
… Well, I'm not going to ask you all of them,
obviously. *(Sighs, puts down NOTEPAD)* Very well
then, what questions do you have for me?
… None whatsoever? I think we see why you
don't work in a creative field.

JACQUI resumes from NOTEPAD, clearing throat.

JACQUI

What sort of tree would you be and why?
… That's not a tree, it's a shrub.

SOUND FX: Bell tinkle.

JACQUI writes a definite cross on CARD, then places PEN down.

JACQUI

That will be all, thank you. You'll be contacted if
you are the successful candidate.

LIGHTS down.

Scene 1.3 – Tom

LIGHTS up.

TOM sits bored at different TABLE with empty PINT glass.

He nods, tries to speak, but can't get a word in, besides "uh huh". He zones out, looking elsewhere, still nodding, as his "Opposite" continues talking.

He makes to drink but realises PINT is empty, then stares sadly at TABLE.

Suddenly, he sits to attention.

TOM

Oh! Right. Hi, I'm Tom.

SOUND FX: Bell tinkle.

TOM

Oh, for fuck's sake.

LIGHTS down.

Scene 1.4 – Meet Chloe

LIGHTS up.

CHLOE is perky but nervously chatterbox, with a score CARD.

CHLOE

Hey there, I'm Chloe. And I'm trying speed dating. *(Waves hands)* Yay for me. Well, you have to try these things.
Singles nights. Online dating. Meetups for people who hate singles nights and online dating. I even tried Speed Bowling. Lawn bowls and dating –

now, that's an afternoon. Though I did win a prize for Best End.

Speed Dinner Parties are another one. Not good for digestion, and *seriously*, make sure you wear a napkin.

So that's me up to date on all the modern dating methods, short of spiking you with Rohypnol. Because, ugh, meeting people in pubs and clubs. The drunken slurring, spilt drinks, inappropriate comments yelled into your ear. And that's just me on vodka.

Joke. Kidding. I hardly ever vomit on people since changing medications. No, joke again.

CHLOE grimaces then changes tack.

CHLOE

I saw this documentary about speed dating recently – not swotting up, just a *really* bad tv night. Apparently, a sense of humour is a plus for guys, but a girl cracking jokes is a real turn-off. Great, so the only novelty I have in my favour is actually totally *not* in my favour.

The theory was that guys don't like girls who make fun of things in case the jokes continue once he gets naked. My theory is, stop providing us with so much material. Or should that be "so little"? Boom-tish!

… You're right, you should do some talking now. So, what do you do besides subjecting yourself to four awkward minutes with complete strangers? And no, that's not another sex joke.

Her "Opposite" comments, deflating her confidence.

CHLOE

No, I wasn't one of the girls in the documentary.
It was actually about first impressions, and how
little it takes to form them. Like how much can
you learn about a person in four minutes?
Enough, for some. Hardly a start for others.

SOUND FX: Bell tinkle.

CHLOE watches as her "Opposite" stands and departs as she speaks.

CHLOE

Then times up, judgements made, and on we
move.
(Calls after her "Opposite") 'Night.

Scene 1.5 – Meet Joanne

JOANNE enters and loiters inconspicuously. Her NAMETAG is a different colour to the others.

CHLOE interprets JOANNE's loitering as a cue to move. She packs up quickly and departs, looking for her next table.

JOANNE checks no one is looking, then swiftly sits at the vacated TABLE. She immediately assumes the demeanour of someone most definitely meant to be here.

Her "Opposite" arrives, receiving a quick efficient smile from JOANNE.

SOUND FX: Bell tinkle.

JOANNE has an urgent edge to her manner.

JOANNE

Right. Hi. I'm Joanne. Jo. Whatever.
Look, I'm actually forty-one and yes, I *should* be
over there in the older group. But fuck, look at
them. They're ancient. That bloke looks like my
dad's golfing partner.
(Ducks down in seat) Shit, I think it is. No, don't
look!
I'm only forty-one! Why am I bundled in with
them? Shunned away in case we taint the young
with our old age germs.

JOANNE keeps her profile low, looking about.

JOANNE

Please don't dob me in! I don't think anyone
noticed me sneak over here, but there's possibly a
girl now looking for her seat. Hi anyway. Nice to
meet you, Andrew.

JOANNE shakes hands with her "Opposite".

JOANNE

It's a bit fucking galling really. We've all paid
significant money to be here tonight, and for the
sake of just thirteen months I'm thrown in with
the Woodstock generation. That's how they
should group this thing. Boomers over there, the
viable breeders here, and Generation Overshare

tucked away in the creche where they can
SnapFace and TwitTok each other to their heart's
content.
I do social media! Well, I look at it. Mostly seems
to be pictures of food then status updates on the
subsequent bowel movements. What happened to
"forty is the new thirty"? We don't suddenly have
a personality bypass at the stroke of midnight.

*JOANNE suddenly covers the side of her face with her hand. She
peeks out.*

JOANNE

God, I really think that is dad's golfing buddy.

SOUND FX: Bell tinkle.

JOANNE reacts like it's an alarm.

JOANNE

Shit, they've found me!
What? Oh, time's up. Thank Christ for that.

*BOUNCER enters, notices JOANNE's NAMETAG then looms
over her.*

JOANNE

No offence, Andrew, you've been lovely. All
twelve or however many years old you are.

Sensing BOUNCER's presence, JOANNE hesitantly looks up.

BOUNCER jerks a thumb for her to move.

JOANNE

Fuck. Rumbled.

LIGHTS down.

Scene 1.6 – Tom Again

LIGHTS up.

TOM sits at another TABLE, looking at a PHOTO.

TOM

Yep, he seems really nice, too. You must be very proud of him.

He sets PHOTO down, but unfortunately his "Opposite" has placed down another.

He picks up another pre-set PHOTO.

TOM

Oh, cool. And how old is he?
… *She.* Right, cool.

He sets PHOTO down, but "Opposite" has placed yet another.

He wearily picks up another pre-set PHOTO.

TOM

Exactly how many cats do you have?

LIGHTS down.

Scene 1.7 – Repetition

LIGHTS up.

MIKE is mid-session at a different TABLE.

MIKE

No, I come along speed dating quite often. I guess the actual chances of finding someone are pretty slim. It's more like an ice-breaking game to give everyone something to talk about over drinks afterwards. *(Thinks)* Maybe I should stick around rather than just leaving.

Anyway, who's to know. On my next table I might meet the love of my life. You might find the next person along is yours. *(Dismayed)* I could be holding you up…

But that's fate for you. It's all luck of a draw. Imagine if you never got to your "One's" table because the event was overbooked. Or your "One" came on a different night or pulled out due to gastro or something.

You'll just have to make do with me in the meantime!

I remember my first speed dating night. I almost lost track of who I was by the end, telling the same old summary of myself over and over. Like

that thing where you repeat a word so many times
it becomes strange and unfamiliar. Only it's your
own name. Just … Michael. Michael.
Michael, Michael, Michael.
And suddenly you're like, who's Michael? What is
this Michael thing?
Michael. Michael.
Michael, Michael, Michael, Michael.
Michael.

SOUND FX: Bell tinkle.

MIKE

Michael, Michael, Michael, Michael.
Yeah, it gets so weird, doesn't it.
Exactly! With common words too. Next, next,
next, next, next, next, next.
… *(Realises)* Oh, right. You mean *next*.
Sorry. Have a great night.

*MIKE makes an obvious tick on CARD, smiles hopefully, then moves
OFF.*

LIGHTS down.

Scene 1.8 – Tom Once More

LIGHTS up.

TOM sits at different TABLE holding TAROT CARDS.

TOM

So, you make *all* your decisions by tarot card?

TOM stares at TAROT CARDS, then wobbles as though affected.

TOM

Actually, I do feel guided towards a decision.

TOM places TAROT CARDS down one by one.

TOM

The Thirsty Man. The Empty Glass. The Bar of
Plenty. And The Giver of No Shits.

*TOM stands, toasts his empty PINT with a friendly nod, then strides
OFF.*

SOUND FX: Bell tinkle.

LIGHTS down.

Scene 1.9 – Chloe's Toilet Friend

LIGHTS up.

CHLOE is mid-session.

CHLOE

A friend of mine just loves speed dating nights.
Until the halftime break.

What do you do? Stick with the girls to compare notes? Chat to the guys you liked so far – or is that too keen? What if they're standing with someone you didn't like – can you ignore one but chat up the other? Or do you approach someone you haven't had a turn with yet? But what if you say something dumb and they cross you off? Or you use up all the topics you'll need with them later, so you end desperately rambling on about nuns or porridge or thrush or something and ruin everything.

No way, don't risk it. My friend says, that is.

So, she just hides in the toilet. Much safer. It's not like it's weird to hang out in a public toilet for twenty minutes. Is it?

I don't know what she gets up to in there. Hair and make-up. Message some people. Pretend to message more people. Chuckle away like you're getting replies. The mobile phone is such a godsend for single people. Probably best not to take any photos though.

(Happy sigh) Nope, that's the way to do it. Stay in the toilets. Cubicle to yourself. Quite relaxing really.

My friend says, that is.

I don't think I could stay there the *entire* interval. Unless maybe I had something dodgy the night before.

CHLOE realises she's rambling, searches for a new topic.

CHLOE

So… do you like curry?

SOUND FX: Bell tinkle.

CHLOE

I've just spent our whole time talking about
toilets, haven't I.
(Bites lip) … Hmm.

LIGHTS down.

Scene 1.10 – Another Question

LIGHTS up.

*JACQUI is in mid-session, reading another question from her
NOTEPAD.*

JACQUI

Would you rather *hands* that kept growing larger
as you got older, or *feet* that kept growing smaller?

JACQUI listens then frowns.

JACQUI

I think it best we ignore you said that.

JACQUI continues frowning, unimpressed.

JACQUI

And that.

LIGHTS down.

Scene 1.11 – In with the Oldies

LIGHTS up.

JOANNE sits, bored and sulking.

JOANNE

No, I don't play golf. My dad does though. Maybe you play at the same club?

JOANNE glances enviously at other tables.

JOANNE

… What? Yes, I am a little distracted.
I was over there earlier. With "the young'uns".
They're a segregated race now. News to me.
Apparently when I woke up last birthday, my Best Before date had expired.
(Indicates herself) Does *this* look past it to you?
(Handles breasts) These babies still pass the pencil test, I can tell you.
… Exactly. I rest my case.

JOANNE looks forlornly to the other tables.

JOANNE

I'm still over there. Mentally. Physically, I'm still packing *quite a bit* of heat. I'm just not ready for … golf.

An idea strikes. JOANNE looks around furtively.

JOANNE

Cover for me. Keep talking about The Gall
Stones, or The Rolling Bladders or whatever
concert you were going on about.

JOANNE sinks down CHAIR, checking that no one is looking.

JOANNE

Keep going, still listening. Sort of. I'm making a
blow for freedom!

JOANNE stops to give her "Opposite" a stern look.

JOANNE

No. An escape.

JOANNE disappears under TABLE, then pops her head up.

JOANNE

Keep talking! Everything's normal.

JOANNE descends under TABLE, then crawls away.

SOUND FX: Various "heys", chairs scraping along, glass breakage.

JOANNE

Sorry.

SOUND FX: Wolf whistle.

JOANNE

Fuck off.

LIGHTS down.

Scene 1.12 – Still Tom

LIGHTS up.

TOM is having another challenging session.

TOM

So, you're vegan…
No, no, I didn't flinch. I just … blinked. With my
entire face.
… Would I be prepared to adopt a vegan lifestyle
if we lived together? And we'd be what – living in
a meat igloo to balance things out? Could I still
have sausages, provided I went down the
driveway and ate them by the letterbox?
… You get really angry for someone who doesn't
eat anywhere near enough protein.

SOUND FX: Bell tinkle.

LIGHTS down.

Scene 1.13 – Jacqui and Mike

LIGHTS up.

MIKE and JACQUI sit at TABLES, performing to audience.

JACQUI has her NOTEPAD. MIKE is borderline terrified.

MIKE

What was the second one again?

JACQUI

(Sighs, reads) White water rafting.

MIKE

D. All of the above.

JACQUI

You can't do all of them on a single date. Besides, I haven't said D yet.

MIKE

Haven't you?

JACQUI

Have you even been listening?

MIKE

I tend to freeze up in exams.

JACQUI

This isn't an exam.

MIKE

It feels like one.

JACQUI

Hot air ballooning.

MIKE

(Pulls at shirt collar) I know, they should open a window or something.

JACQUI

No. Option D.

MIKE

Okay, option D.

JACQUI

No. I am saying that option D is "Hot Air Ballooning".

MIKE

What was the first one again?

JACQUI

I'm not telling you again. You should have listened.

MIKE

Can't we just talk?

JACQUI

We are talking.

MIKE

This feels more like you're telling me off. You're very assertive.

JACQUI

Are you calling me bossy?

MIKE

God no, I wouldn't dare.

JACQUI

Some of my work *associates* once called me bossy.
I reported them to my manager.

MIKE

What did he do?

JACQUI

I told him he had to reprimand them.

MIKE

And did he?

JACQUI

He did after I escalated things to the Company
Director. I got my apology then! And one from
my work colleagues. There was even talk of
promotion to a division of my own.

MIKE

Of your own, or *on* your own?

JACQUI

… Just answer the question.

MIKE

I've forgotten what it was.

JACQUI

What are you, a goldfish?

MIKE

Was that the question?

JACQUI

What possible reason would I ask you that for?

MIKE

We really don't seem to be hitting it off.

JACQUI

Only because you keep doing it wrong. There's still time to improve.

MIKE

I think I heard the bell.

JACQUI

Just pick an answer.

MIKE

C.

JACQUI

Are you just guessing?

MIKE

… no.

JACQUI

What was C?

MIKE

Don't you remember?

JACQUI

I don't have to, it's written here in front of me.

MIKE

Well, there you go then.

JACQUI

Are you just saying C in the hope I'll move on to the next question?

MIKE

There's more?

JACQUI

We'll keep going till you get them right and we match.

MIKE

Do you really think we will?

JACQUI

With appropriate direction, you might. What's your ideal holiday destination? A – a five-star beachside hotel?

MIKE

(Grabs PEN) Can I write them down this time?

SOUND FX: Bell tinkle.

JACQUI

Look, just give me my tick and we'll sort it out
later.

JACQUI stands, then addresses an "Organiser".

JACQUI

Excuse me. Do we get free bottled water or is it
only from the tap?
(Hears answer) Oh for pity's sake!

JACQUI departs.

Shell-shocked, MIKE looks at his CARD, shrugs, then ticks.

LIGHTS down.

Scene 1.14 – More Peas, Dear?

LIGHTS up.

CHLOE is very enamoured with her current "Opposite".

CHLOE

What sort of guy do I like? Would "any" sound
too desperate?
… Yes, I suppose it does. Obviously, someone
attractive. *(Leans in, flirty)* Like your good self.
Muscular. *(Leans in, flirty)* Like your good self.
Intelligent and well-spoken. Like your good self
again.

I think we're starting to see a bit of a pattern here! Then the usual stuff. Kind, independent. Virile. *(Hand to mouth jokingly)* Oops! Did I just say that?
Good relationship with their family.
Though not to the point that we're going over every weekend to your folks for dinner, dealing with your racist dad, and your drunk depressed auntie, and your little brother who gets a little too visibly excited at seeing a grown female. And the dog that always barks at me, yet never did that for that other girl you used to bring home. Yes, she probably did have a friendlier face. And your mum's mistaken slips of that ex-girlfriend's name, just a few too many times to be just an accident. Or indeed, actually inviting that ex-girlfriend on over because everyone loved her *so much*, including the fucking dog. Well, she's like one of the family now, isn't she. The daughter we so *very nearly* had. So *very* nearly. Will anyone ever quite live up to her? "He looks and looks, but will he ever find?" Oh, more peas dear?

CHLOE realises her escalated energy level and composes herself.

CHLOE

Just a story a friend told me.
And my ideal man needs to have brown eyes.
Don't know why, I just have a thing for them.
Like your good- …
… Hazel? Are you sure?
(Leans forward squinting) And they've always been like that? Not some trick of the light?

(Sits back) Oh. Well, obviously, that isn't a deal breaker.

Conflicted, CHLOE peers again, then sits back and taps her CARD on the TABLE.

CHLOE

You could always wear coloured contacts. No? … Oh. No.

SOUND FX: Bell tinkle.

CHLOE

Okay, bye.

CHLOE waves as "Opposite" departs then sits back, glum.

CHLOE

I fucking hate peas.

LIGHTS down.

Scene 1.15 – Jacqui's Ideal Date

LIGHTS up.

JACQUI is reading another question from her NOTEPAD.

JACQUI

Question Three: What is your ideal date night for us?

A) a fancy restaurant that's the talk of the town.
B) the latest show at the theatre.
C) the local speedway for a night of "racing mayhem". *(Gives disapproving face)*
Or D) a mystery voyage to sample wines, local produce, and hidden away art galleries.
… Okay, and a brewery then. But we'd have to stop at a cheese shop to even things up.
… It doesn't matter which date. First, second, or third.
… No, there isn't a "none of the above".
Well, try. Surely all of your dates don't just end up at your place after the pub.
… I'll ignore that.
… It's not stupid. It's a perfectly valid questionnaire. I have to say evasiveness isn't a very endearing trait in a potential partner.
Or one who sulks.
… Or gives deliberately contrary answers. It's quite simple. A, B, C or D.
Yes, I am prepared to wait our time out if I must.
There's no point asking another question if you won't answer the last.

JACQUI folds her arms adamantly.

JACQUI

Well, two can play at that game. Rather immature if you ask me.
You *are* immature.
I'm not immature, you are. Sticking your tongue out only confirms it.
It's a shame, you seemed quite nice when you said hello.

SOUND FX: Bell tinkle.

JACQUI

Time's up. Thank you.
… So, what is your answer?

NUDE GUY rushes ON, behind an oblivious JACQUI, with underpants on his head – presumably his own.

NUDE GUY

Wa-hey! Bits out for the ladies!

NUDE GUY tears OFF, chased by BOUNCER.

A beat.

JACQUI

… What nude guy?

LIGHTS down.

Scene 1.16 – Modern Mobile Etiquette

LIGHTS up.

JOANNE sits, frustrated by the conversation in progress.

JOANNE

Let's try music. What do you listen to?

… And that's a genre? Sounds more like a list of
adjectives. What about actual bands?
… Nope. Never heard of them.
… Yes, they do sound very "authentic".
… Banjos, really? So, you go to live music gigs?
… I suppose, technically, a DJ is "live". But I
meant with instruments. And actual skill, talent
and effort.
(Finally, a connection) Yes! I go to music festivals
too! Or used to. They're quite a long day without
seating.
… Yes, very *authentic* experiences, though. You've
quite the *authentic* hipster look there yourself. That
is a *significant* amount of braiding for a beard. And
a significant amount of beard. Who'd have
thought the Ned Kelly look would come back in
style. Not so far as putting a bucket on your head
as yet, but hey, who knows.

SOUND FX: *SMS message.*

JOANNE

Oh. Sure. Check your message.

JOANNE sits back, unimpressed.

JOANNE

I'm sure it must be something *very* important for
you to ignore all concept of conversational
protocol.

*JOANNE ducks down as BOUNCER walks through, glancing her
way.*

Her "Opposite" finishes with their phone.

JOANNE

Funny one, was it?
… Sexting? *(Wryly curious)* No, I've never actually
been sent a "sext".
… Okay. "Bluetooth" me in then.

*JOANNE pushes her MOBILE forward, watches her "Opposite" do
something, then picks up MOBILE and struggles to make out the
picture.*

JOANNE

What is it? *(Realises)* Is that yours?
You braid down *there* as well?

She looks again, confused.

JOANNE

It looks like Captain Jack Sparrow.

JOANNE sits back, deflated.

JOANNE

Oh, grow up.

SOUND FX: Bell tinkle.

LIGHTS down.

Scene 1.17 – Ships in the Night

LIGHTS up.

MIKE sits at TABLE, confused by the "Opposite" sitting down before him.

MIKE

… Hi. I'm Mike.

MIKE offers a wary hand, shakes.

MIKE

… Right. Okay.
… Well, hi Colin.

Awkward pause.

MIKE

I think one of us might have the wrong table.

LIGHTS down.

Scene 1.18 – Tom Meets Jacqui

LIGHTS up.

JACQUI sits at one TABLE, TOM at another. It is their turn together, but still facing the audience.

JACQUI

(Gathers NOTEPAD) Now, if you keep your answers short, we should get through most of my questions.

TOM

Do you want my urine sample now or afterwards?

JACQUI

The questions will assist conversation, while also determining our match potential.

TOM

They must be good questions.

JACQUI

They're very good questions. *(Reads)* What would you consider your worst characteristic?

TOM

That's a terrible question.

JACQUI

What's wrong with it?

TOM

I'd prefer to name my best characteristic.

JACQUI

Why are you so keen to hide your worst characteristic?

TOM

I'd rather put my best foot forward than my worst.

JACQUI

It reveals how honest you are.

TOM

What if I just said I'm honest?

JACQUI

As your best or worst characteristic?

TOM

Depends on what I'm being honest about.

JACQUI

I'm putting down "evasive".

TOM

(Shrugs) It's your list.

JACQUI

These questions were devised by a respected psychologist.

TOM

Did they get laid as a result of using them?

JACQUI

They'd hardly be respected if they did. They're about gauging compatibility, not "getting laid".

TOM

You're telling me.

JACQUI

You're obviously another oaf with no regard for the scientific method. Let's quit right here.

TOM

Fine by me.

They both cross arms and sit in silence.

JACQUI

Well, off you go then.

TOM

I'm comfortable here. You move.

JACQUI

The men move. The ladies stay. I'm not budging an inch.

TOM

Neither am I.

They sit, then JACQUI picks up her NOTEPAD.

JACQUI

We may as well continue my questions then.

TOM immediately stands.

TOM

Okay, I'll go. … If you're okay with everyone wondering why I left you.

JACQUI

Obviously because you're rude and arrogant.

TOM

Or you're so unbearable I bailed out early. Bad look.

JACQUI considers, then stands.

JACQUI

Not if I bail on you first.

TOM sits down, smiling with satisfaction.

TOM

Goodo. Have a nice night.

JACQUI hovers, not wanting to be outsmarted.

JACQUI

It looks *much* worse if a girl walks away.

TOM

No, it doesn't. You'll just look moody.

JACQUI

They'll think you're some axe murderer.

TOM

A very comfortably seated axe murderer. I think
I'll live.

JACQUI turns CHAIR around, then sits with her back to him.

TOM

Are you ignoring me?

JACQUI

Sure am.

TOM

For the next two minutes?

JACQUI

I've ignored people for much longer than that.

TOM

I'm sure you have.

*Feeling impudent, TOM tears some BAR MAT, quickly chews it into
a ball, then flicks it "at" JACQUI, providing his own warfare sound
effect.*

JACQUI reacts as though something has hit the back of her neck.

JACQUI

Ignoring you.

*TOM tears another strip and chews, as JACQUI wriggles – the spitball
fell down her top.*

JACQUI whirls round. TOM immediately stops chewing.

JACQUI

Was that beer or spit?

Caught out, TOM speaks with the wad in his mouth.

TOM

Probably beer.

JACQUI

What's in your mouth?

TOM forces himself to swallow.

TOM

Probably beer.

JACQUI

Do you want me to call security?

TOM

Is that one of your questions?

JACQUI

I'll have you thrown out.

TOM

I don't want to be here anyway.

JACQUI

That makes two of us. I don't want you here
either.

TOM

Any potential partners survived your interrogation so far?

JACQUI

I'm getting answers.

TOM

Are most of them "No"?

JACQUI

They are if I'm answering to you.

They sit in silence.

TOM

You know, you're the most fun four minutes I've had all evening.

JACQUI

Really?

TOM

Yep. That's how bad a night it's been.

JACQUI scowls but relents.

JACQUI

… So has mine.

TOM

See. *Now* we're being honest.

SOUND FX: Bell tinkle.

TOM

So, what's your worst characteristic?

JACQUI

People seem to think I'm uptight.

TOM

(Mock surprise) Really?

LIGHTS down.

Scene 1.19 – Chloe and Mike

SOUND FX: Bell tinkle.

LIGHTS up.

MICHAEL sits at a TABLE, CHLOE at another TABLE nearby.

It appears to be their turn together, but they are actually in separate conversations.

MIKE

Michael. *(Points at nametag)* Or "Mike".

CHLOE

I'm Chloe.

MIKE

Pretty *mad* evening so far.

CHLOE

Four minutes is so quick. Or *sooo* long, in some cases!

MIKE

Hopefully, I'll be an improvement on your last person.

CHLOE

Not to put pressure on. I'm not like "Grr, entertain me!".

MIKE

Well, I *do* have quite a few stories to tell. …
They've all just slipped my mind, but I'm sure one will come to me.

CHLOE

I'm pretty easy going. Low maintenance. Though I don't slop around in my trackies all day. Well, not *all* day.

MIKE

Sorry, I don't quite get what you mean.

CHLOE

No, no. My mistake.

MIKE

Oh! Right.

CHLOE

That's us off to an awkward start. Well, the only way is up!

MIKE

I was probably watching something on the other channel.

CHLOE

Apologies already. We'll be having crazy make-up sex next.

MIKE

That's exactly how I love spending my free time.

CHLOE

That wasn't actually an invite.

MIKE

Though I did sprain an ankle once. I'm not very coordinated.

CHLOE

My friend gave me a lift here, so I'll stick with her.

MIKE

Since then, no more salsa dancing for me.

CHLOE

I'm sure your flat is really cool.

MIKE

Hey, I like the Macarena too!
… Oh, you're being ironic.

CHLOE

No, I'll pass on the Netflix and chill.

An awkward lull. MIKE and CHLOE both sip their DRINKS.

CHLOE

At least this is better than online dating.

MIKE

Online dating is terrible, isn't it.

CHLOE

I mean, I suppose it's fun.

MIKE

It does have a few good points.

CHLOE

Or maybe I just like filling in forms.

MIKE

I never know what to say.

CHLOE

Like a Christmas wish list, putting down what you
want – eyes, hair colour, height.

MIKE

I try not being too particular.

CHLOE

It made me think about what I was *actually* looking for.

MIKE

I'm not sure who I'm looking for.

CHLOE

Do I really want someone who listens to Cold Chisel on a regular basis?

MIKE

Smokers were definitely out.

CHLOE

Could I demand qualities that I didn't actually have myself?

MIKE

And nail-biters. Their own or others'.

CHLOE

I'm prepared to overlook quite a bit.

MIKE

And I'm really not sure about dogs.

CHLOE

Though they have to be a good kisser.

MIKE

All that slobbering and licking. It's gross.

CHLOE

But you can't put that on your profile.

MIKE & CHLOE

People have said I'm quite the catch.

MIKE

And not just my mum.

CHLOE

But it all seemed like "Judgemental dotcom". Swish left and strike them out as soon as they don't tick a box.

MIKE

That sounds really painful.

CHLOE

Are we the best judge of what we want?

MIKE

I hate going to the dentist.

CHLOE

Like when you meet someone but despite all the differences and incompatibilities, something just clicks.

MIKE

"Spit" they say, then get really mad if you miss the basin.

CHLOE

Like cooking, where you hate all the ingredients, but it turns out to be your new favourite dish.

MIKE

Sometimes I feel numb without the anaesthetic.

CHLOE

(*Flails PENCIL absent-mindedly*) So why do we keep these impossible checklists? Where's the serendipity?

CHLOE accidentally drops PENCIL on floor between TABLES.

MIKE instinctively leans over to pick it up. CHLOE stops before they butt heads.

He offers the PENCIL to her. A moment. Serendipity.

MIKE

Here you go.

CHLOE

Oh. Thanks.

They return to their independent conversations but affected by their interaction.

MIKE AND CHLOE

So, where were we?

CHLOE

(Disappointed) No. I'm not a fan of fast food.

MIKE

You have *two* dogs?

SOUND FX: Bell tinkle.

CHLOE

That was great. Have a great night.

MIKE

I had a blast, too. … Or are you being ironic
again?

CHLOE

Get a drink together? Nah. That's not how this
works.

*Having made another obvious tick on his CARD, MIKE gathers his
DRINK, CARD and PEN and stands.*

… as CHLOE gathers her things and stands.

Turning, CHLOE and MIKE come face to face.

They hover, unable to break the ice, then swap TABLES and sit.

*MIKE looks to CHLOE in confusion, then turns to his new
"Opposite".*

MIKE

Have things got out of order?

CHLOE looks over, sees MIKE has already begun with his new "Opposite". She offers her hand to her new "Opposite".

CHLOE

Chloe.

MIKE looks to CHLOE, sees her shaking hands.

SOUND FX: Bell tinkle.

They turn to their new "Opposites".

MIKE & CHLOE

So, what do you do for fun?

LIGHTS down.

Scene 1.20 – Night of the Cougar

LIGHTS up.

JOANNE leans forward at a TABLE with menace.

JOANNE

No, *really*. Define *cougar* exactly.

JOANNE listens to "Opposite's" reply, then sits back, satisfied with the apology.

JOANNE

And even mention biological clock again, I *will* glass you.

SOUND FX: SMS arrives on JOANNE's MOBILE.

JOANNE looks at her MOBILE, then recoils.

JOANNE

For fuck's sake.

JOANNE glares, looking around for the culprit.

JOANNE

(Shouts) And that goes for you too, Captain Jack!

BOUNCER enters, then looms over JOANE's shoulder.

Sensing a presence, JOANNE looks up innocently.

JOANNE

Have you seen my twin *older* sister? She's round here somewhere.

BOUNCER slowly shakes head.

Defeated, JOANNE stands and walks OFF with BOUNCER.

LIGHTS down.

Scene 1.21 – Finally, Meet Tom

SOUND FX: Bell tinkle.

LIGHTS up.

TOM at TABLE reacts with surprise.

TOM

I can start? Oh. Okay. Wow.
Well, I'm Tom, and I'm here because my friends tricked me. "Come for a drink" they said, then lo and behold, I'm steered up here, booked and paid for in advance. Then they swan off downstairs to make sure I don't run away.
I have to pay their drinks tab if I try.
So, here I am – against my will. Single, but not actually looking. Think of me as a time-out. A chaser between drinks.
… Yeah, it was a recent break up. Well guessed. Well, recent-*ish*. There are some who say enough time has passed. They're mostly downstairs getting pissed and laughing at my expense. Others – pretty much just me actually – say not quite yet.
… Oh, the usual "it's-not-you-it's-me-but-the-*me*-that-requires-*you*-to-*not*-be-with-me-and-the-*we*-to-be-a-*not-us*-any-more" kind of thing.
Yeah, that old chestnut.
… Sure, I *might* meet someone tonight. But that would need some sort of blinding flash from the blue. And realistically, they don't really happen. Sometimes "moving on" needs some time alone. Besides, it's unfair to any new person, competing

against some lingering "greatest hits" of an ideal
someone who really doesn't exist anymore.
Or maybe never did.
So, blinding flashes aside, better to bide time
getting used to things being in the past tense,
then come at things fresh. No benchmarks of
perfect false memories. And hopefully no speed
dating nights.
… No. Probably not tonight.
Anyway, we're breaking the cardinal rule: No
Talking About Exes. So, no more of that.

His "Opposite" asks a question.

TOM

… Do I miss her?
Yeah. I still miss her.

SOUND FX: Bell tinkle.

LIGHTS down.

Scene 1.22 – Chloe and Abigail

LIGHTS up.

CHLOE sits at a TABLE, already chatting away.

CHLOE

I wasn't brave enough on my first speed dating
night, so I convinced my friend Abigail to come
with me.

Abby is *gorgeous*. Easily could've been a model. But guys won't approach her, probably assuming someone that stunning will knock them back. Besides, of course I would bring a totally hot friend to an event where we're essentially competing for men? As I soon realised, standing around beforehand, with *all* eyes on her. Even the girls seemed interested. One guy asked her out, like a sort of pre-emptive strike.

Anyway, the bell rings, and off we start. First thing *every* guy asks me is if I came along with Abigail. They all know her name already! One guy doesn't even bother writing me down on his card. All he can talk about is Abby. And sure, Abby *is* amazing, but you're supposed to be getting to know *me*.

CHLOE grabs "Opposite's" hand.

CHLOE

Suddenly, he grabs my hand, pleading "Honestly Helen, I need to know…"
(Points to NAMETAG, correcting) Chloe.
"Do I have a chance with Abigail?" he begs. And Abby looks over, wondering why this guy and I are staring at her, hand in hand. The bloke she's with already looks about to leap to one knee and propose.
So, I ask: "What am I? Chopped liver?" And it's like he's only just noticed I'm female. And he says "You're … okay, Helen."
(Points to NAMETAG, insisting) Chloe!
"You seem really nice," he says, then gazes away at Abby until the bell goes.

And that's the thing. I'm "okay". Nice little Chloe.
Not gorgeous. Not a knock-out. Certainly no
Abigail.
I'm not even a Helen.
I'm me. And surely someone must think that's
worth a try.
I'd do me if I were that way inclined. Or flexible
enough.
So, you start to question, looking for the flaws
and defects. And they must exist, because there's
got to be a reason why this whole-lot-of-nothing
keeps happening.
So, you find them. The faults, real or otherwise.
Anything. Everything. Blowing your confidence
all the more.
Until finally you realise: "Oh god, I'm the
Personality Girl, aren't I." The one that mums
and aunts set up with their "Personality" Sons
and Nephews. The one that gets whole nights of
guys asking me to put a good word in for them
with Abby.
… Like I've spent four minutes talking about her
now.
Just for once, I want someone to talk about me.
To *want* me. Not Abby. Not Helen. Just me.
Just once.
… What? *(Sighs)* No, you can't have Abby's
number.

SOUND FX: Bell tinkle.

CHLOE

Oh, thank fuck, it's the interval.

LIGHTS down.

54

ACT TWO

Scene 2.1 – Interval

SOUND FX: Background music – something sleazy but cheesy.

LIGHTS up.

One TABLE now has BOWL OF NUTS.

TOILET SIGN hangs on rear wall/curtain, towards one side.

TOM enters with PINT. He warily eyes the "Crowd".

With no intention to mix, he seeks out the furthest TABLE. He sits on far CHAIR to watch a "TV" mounted on the "wall".

MIKE enters with brightly coloured COCKTAIL. He eyes the "Crowd", daunted by the thought of socialising. He nervously sips his drink.

Noticing TOM, MIKE sidles over to hover in hope of invitation to conversation. Unaware, TOM continues watching "TV".

MIKE grabs nearby CHAIR to sit with TOM.

TOM becomes aware of MIKE sitting close by.

MIKE nods a greeting then sips COCKTAIL.

TOM regards the COCKTAIL then returns attention to "TV". He shifts his CHAIR along for more personal space.

JACQUI enters, HANDBAG on arm, unimpressed with her frozen COCKTAIL.

Seeing TOM and MIKE, JACQUI immediately moves away in disgust to nearby TABLE with BOWL OF NUTS.

Receiving no interaction from TOM, MIKE looks around. He spots JACQUI. Reacting with terror, he angles his CHAIR away from her, closer to TOM.

TOM pointedly shuffles his CHAIR from MIKE to maintain distance, adamantly favouring the "TV" with his attention.

CHLOE enters with COCKTAIL to loiter, sheepishly sipping her drink. Since MIKE's back is to her, she doesn't notice him.

A long enough pause such that the audience also feel the excruciating awkwardness of the total lack of communication on stage.

Finally, CHLOE approaches JACQUI.

CHLOE

Excuse me. Do you know where the toilets are?

JACQUI

Given the organisation so far, they probably don't have any.

CHLOE

Seriously?

JACQUI

(Points) Over there, I think.

CHLOE

Oh. Right, thanks.

CHLOE moves to the TOILET SIGN but stops to give her surroundings one more look. Nope, it's all too confronting. She darts OFF to the toilet.

MIKE stirs his COCKTAIL as TOM drinks his PINT.

They regard the other's drink choices. MIKE takes a manly sip through STRAW.

MIKE nods at "TV" above them.

MIKE

Who's winning?

TOM

Beats me.

MIKE

Who's playing?

TOM

(Points to "TV") Those guys, and … those guys.

MIKE

Not a football fan?

TOM

Not especially.

MIKE

Having fun tonight?

TOM

Not especially.

MIKE gives an experienced nod and sigh.

MIKE

No luck so far, eh?

TOM

And getting worse by the second.

MIKE

Take my tip. Tick "yes" for every girl. Guaranteed a win.

TOM

That's a bit desperate, isn't it?

MIKE

… Some guy over there told me.

TOM

What if none of them tick you back?

MIKE

You get a discount voucher for next time. … So
I've heard.

*MIKE takes a defensive sip on his COCKTAIL as TOM regards his
knowledge with suspicion.*

*JOANNE pokes her head in. The coast clear, she enters with
HANDBAG and COCKTAIL. She is pleased with her stealth —
back in with the younger group again!*

*Struggling to drink her frozen COCKTAIL, JOANNE approaches
JACQUI.*

JOANNE

We'll hardly get drunk if the drinks are frozen
solid.

JACQUI

They're not alcoholic.

JOANNE

You're kidding?

JACQUI

I wouldn't be drinking one if they were.

JOANNE

What's the point of a free non-alcoholic drink?
Spice 'em up, get everyone breaking the ice.

JACQUI

It says little for people if they require alcohol to interact. Natural personality should shine out.

JOANNE dubiously regards JACQUI's less-than-vibrant personality.

JOANNE

I should've brought my sunglasses.

JACQUI

There's already been one drunk evicted for lewd behaviour. What a waste of an entrance fee.

JOANNE jabs at COCKTAIL while speaking, making little progress.

JOANNE

He probably didn't pay one. These things are always short of guys, so they round some up from the bar at the last minute.

JACQUI

So, *we're* paying significant money to meet men we could've met at the bar anyway?

JOANNE

Or would've avoided at the bar. Here we get to pay to be hit on instead.

JACQUI

I hate bars. They're loud, smelly and full of drunks.

JOANNE

I'd have thought guys would jump at the chance to safely approach *fifteen* single women. *(Shouts)* If you could hear over the background music!

BOUNCER passes through sternly. JOANNE shrinks to avoid being seen.

JACQUI

Guys who talk to me are only ever interested in one thing.

JOANNE

(Gives JACQUI a glance over, joking) The football score?

JACQUI

Yes, funnily enough. … I'm not sure why.

JOANNE

Maybe they mistook you for an umpire.

JACQUI

No, a goalpost, according to one.

JOANNE refrains from comment. They stab at their frozen COCKTAILS.

JOANNE

What a night. Paying to meet some bar blokes and a complimentary ice slushy.

JACQUI

That's not very "glass half full" of you.

JOANNE

Mine's frozen over.

MIKE gives up looking around for CHLOE. He ponders sharing his angst with TOM…

… just as CHLOE returns with renewed courage to attempt socialising!

Her courage wilts. She sneaks back OFF to the toilet.

MIKE

I think I met a girl.

TOM

Just the one?

MIKE

You think she could be The One?

TOM

The whole idea is to meet *lots* of girls. You sure you're doing this properly?

MIKE

We sort of bumped into each other, in-between rounds.

TOM

Did you get her name while bumping in-betweens?

MIKE

I didn't think to ask.

TOM

Didn't you read her nametag?

MIKE

I was too busy looking at her.

TOM

Why didn't you talk while you had the chance?

MIKE

It wasn't our turn. Maybe we'll meet in the second half.

TOM

Unless she left because idiots like you didn't talk to her.

MIKE

But we haven't finished.

TOM

People can leave. Why stick around if you're having a crap time? *(Frowns)* Why am *I* sticking around?

MIKE

But that would throw everything out of order.

TOM

It's already out of order after the nude guy.

MIKE

Nude guy? What, like a floor show?

TOM

Some drunk dude whose chat up line was "Wanna see my willy". Then it escalated. The chat up line, that is.

MIKE

That's a relief.

TOM

Not for the girl he stripped off for. She's been in tears ever since.

MIKE

Oh, her! I thought she wasn't very talkative.

TOM

Didn't you ask her why she was crying?

MIKE

I just assumed it was something I said. ...

TOM frowns at MIKE.

MIKE

… It's quicker that way.

TOM

You *really* aren't doing this properly, are you.

JACQUI and JOANNE are prodding frozen COCKTAILS with STRAWS.

JACQUI

It's the immaturity that disappoints me.

JOANNE

I only wish for immaturity. The only eligible thing my bachelors are for is the pension.

JACQUI

I doubt any of mine had steady jobs, either.

JOANNE

I meant the age pension. *(Confesses)* I'm in with the over 40's. *(Points at differently coloured NAMETAG)* And in answer to your next question: I know I don't look over 40.

JACQUI looks blankly as JOANNE waits for the expected reply.

JOANNE

(Pointedly) I know I don't look over 40.

JACQUI obliviously prods her COCKTAIL.

JACQUI

You're probably better off. The men my age are *so* juvenile.

JOANNE

Juvenile would be a blessing. You try arthritic.

JACQUI

It's perfectly clear the only thing they want from me is sex.

JOANNE discreetly sucks at her COCKTAIL but recoils with a brain freeze. JACQUI sees her reaction.

JACQUI

Yes, I know, shocking isn't it. I detest them all.

JOANNE manages to defrost her head.

JOANNE

Ooh, that's cold.

JACQUI

Maybe I am. But I want mature. A gentleman who knows how to woo. Sex should be the last thing to cross their mind.

JOANNE

If some of mine had sex it probably would be the last thing that crossed their mind.

JACQUI

It's typical of the organisation tonight. They've put us in completely the wrong groups.

Stabbing their COCKTAILS, they look to the other as the same idea strikes.

MIKE is looking around with increasing frustration.

TOM

You *really* want to meet someone tonight.

MIKE

Don't you?

TOM

I dunno. Eventually. Maybe.

MIKE

Better decide quick. There's only eight more rounds to go.

TOM

Eight! Fucking hell.

MIKE

It'll be over in a flash and then where will you be?

TOM

Free? Happy?

MIKE

Back at home, regretting your missed opportunities.

TOM

And where will you be?

MIKE

Generally, after these things, back at home regretting my missed opportunities.

TOM

You ever considered other methods of meeting women?

MIKE

Depends how much the joining fee is.

TOM

No, I mean just getting out and meeting people.

MIKE

So … not in a pre-arranged, structured meet-up with a minimum guaranteed conversation time? *(Considers, shakes head)* No, it's just a matter of the right tactic.

TOM

How about withdrawal? I'm not ready for any of this.

MIKE

Where would you be otherwise?

TOM

… probably at home, regretting missed opportunities.

MIKE

(Deflates) Exactly. Fifteen rounds of them.

TOM

No. Just one.

JOANNE and JACQUI swap their differently coloured NAMETAGS, pinning them as they talk. JACQUI is unsure.

JOANNE

Well, *I* think it'll work. Something has to work.

JACQUI

It's against the rules.

JOANNE

Sod the rules We're actually doing the organiser's job – putting ourselves in the categories that best suit us.

JACQUI produces CARD from HANDBAG.

JACQUI

But our scorecards …

JOANNE swaps JACQUI's CARD with her own.

JOANNE

We can exchange any matches later.

JACQUI

We can screen each other's candidates. *(Eager)* I've got just the questions for vetting out riff raff.

JOANNE

Maybe just pass on the numbers. *(Pulls out MOBILE)* Now, give me your contact details.

JOANNE is dismayed by a new message.

JACQUI leans over and frowns at the screen.

JACQUI

Why do you have a penis as a screensaver?

JOANNE

It's a message. From a jerk. And his friends have joined in. Unless his does impersonations. Give me a sec to tell him to shove it up his arse.

JOANNE begins typing a furious message.

JACQUI

Is it from an ex?

JOANNE

From a never-was, and never-will-be.

JACQUI

Why did you give him your number?

JOANNE

I didn't! He did that … blue-rooting, or whatever it's called.

JACQUI

I've never heard of that.

JOANNE

He just waggled his near mine then next I know, he was in and up to no good.

JACQUI

(Horrified) And you just let him?

JOANNE

I didn't know he had done it until too late.

JACQUI

I hoped you used protection.

JOANNE

Just a passcode. I thought that was enough. But unfortunately, he found a back door.

JACQUI pulls out HAND SANITISER for a quick cleanse …

… as JOANNE triumphantly presses SEND.

JOANNE

Done.

JACQUI

What if the organisers discover we've swapped?

JOANNE

We tell them we're paying customers, and the customer is always right. From now on, you're Joanne and I'm Jacqui.

JACQUI

But people will notice our ages are hugely different.

JOANNE gives JACQUI an icy look.

JOANNE

No, they won't. We're practically twins.

CHLOE apprehensively wanders ON again.

An idea! She whips out MOBILE PHONE and pretends to be on a call with animated facial reactions.

It feels fake. She bites her lip then darts back OFF to the toilets.

MIKE

Do you have any tips for tonight?

TOM

Run while you can?

MIKE

Dating tips, not …survival.

TOM

I dunno. Be yourself?

MIKE

God no. I've heard the idea is to be *intriguing*.
Mysterious. Put questions in their head.

TOM

"Is he on medication?" … "Would he catch me if
I made a run for it?"

MIKE

Not those sorts of questions.

TOM

Actually, that was just me thinking out loud.

MIKE

I've heard of one technique. Neg Hits. They're
like backhanded compliments. Say something nice
but with a negative twist.

TOM

So … insulting them?

MIKE

But as a compliment. It makes you a challenge.

TOM

Mentally challenged?

MIKE

Exactly. Psychological. It works best on girls who usually get lots of compliments already. They think, "Hey, this guy throwing little hand grenades at me – he's kinda confident."

TOM

"And kind of a douchebag."

MIKE

Some guys say it's the sure way to pick up hot women.

TOM

Such as emergency room nurses when you regain consciousness from being slapped?

MIKE

I read about it online.

TOM

Oh, it must be true then.

The girls are checking their appearances – JACQUI with HAND MIRROR, JOANNE with COMPACT.

JACQUI

I'm not sure I can pull off "over forty".

JOANNE

You're fine. Most of them are losing their eyesight anyway.

JACQUI

I'll put on extra make up. Like I have more to
hide.

*JOANNE reacts but decides to wind back her make-up instead.
Satisfied, she closes her COMPACT.*

JOANNE

Luckily, I have no worries pulling off "under
forty".

JACQUI avoids JOANNE's gaze with a non-committal "mmm".

JOANNE opens COMPACT to check her reflection once more.

JACQUI

Old men get called "distinguished". What's our
equivalent of "The Silver Fox"?

JOANNE

"The Hungry Cougar".

*JACQUI instinctively offers JOANNE a nearby BOWL OF
NUTS.*

JOANNE

(Unimpressed) No thank you.

JACQUI

So, are you divorced?

JOANNE

No.

JACQUI

Separated?

JOANNE

No.

JACQUI

Widowed?

JOANNE

… I'm only a little older than you.

JACQUI

Bit more than a little.

JOANNE

I'm just like you– … *(Regards JACQUI) Quite* like you. Living life, looking for someone right. Then bang – up comes forty. No warning. Suddenly gravity brings you down to a whole different planet. Believe me, watch out.

JACQUI

I doubt it'll be an issue. I've always been mature for my age. My high school boyfriend said going out with me was like dating his aunty.

JOANNE stifles her reaction to just a raised eyebrow.

JACQUI

A very sensible and proper lady. And absolutely the best Bridge partner I've ever played with.

JOANNE

You played Bridge in high school?

JACQUI

We still catch up for the odd quick hand.

JOANNE

Your high school boyfriend?

JACQUI

No, his aunt. She makes the most wonderful lavender scones.

JOANNE

I'm not sure the over-forties will be quite old enough for you.

MIKE is looking around, restless.

MIKE

We can't both do the "Mystery Moody Guy in the corner" thing. People will think it's agoraphobics' night.

TOM

I'm not doing a "thing". Just waiting for it all to be over.

MIKE notices JOANNE glancing in their vicinity.

MIKE

It's working though. Girls are looking at you.

TOM

Maybe they're looking at you.

MIKE waves at JOANNE, but she's gazing elsewhere.

MIKE

No. It's you, with all your playing hard-to-get.

TOM

I'm not playing hard-to-get.

MIKE

When I do that, people think I'm sulking or recently bereaved. Instead, you're swatting them away like flies.

JOANNE takes a big sip of her COCKTAIL. Brain freeze!

TOM

They're not remotely interested.

JOANNE turns their way, wide-eyed with a frozen cerebrum.

MIKE

(Points) That one can barely take her eyes off you.

TOM

Where?

TOM looks but JOANNE has turned, tapping her head in spasmodic recovery.

MIKE

Now she's giggling about you looking back. This is so unfair!

TOM

I'm not doing anything!

MIKE

Exactly! You're on fire, dude. If this were a casino, I'd bet wherever you put your chips. Unless it's roulette. I have a thing about the ball flinging out and choking someone.

TOM

(Considering) People have said it was time I moved on.

MIKE

If not tonight, then when? Any other time, people would just think you're some anti-social arsehole.

TOM

Thanks.

MIKE

But tonight … *you da man.* Anyway, I'm giving it a try.

TOM

Being an anti-social arsehole?

MIKE

No. Neg Hits. Being a challenge by giving sly put-downs.

TOM

So basically, being an anti-social arsehole.

MIKE

Yeah, but a really self-confident one. You think it'll work?

TOM

I think you'll get drinks thrown in your face.

MIKE

Well, *I* think it'll work. Something has to work.

SOUND FX: Bell tinkle.

JOANNE

Seriously, are we doing this?

JACQUI comes to a decision.

JACQUI

Let's do it.

JOANNE

Good luck!

JOANNE and JACQUI pat the other's arm, then depart.

MIKE pops his collar.

TOM

Seriously, are you doing that?

MIKE gives him "pistol fingers".

MIKE

Let's do it!

TOM

Good luck …

TOM and MIKE depart, as BOUNCER enters to set any CHAIRS and props.

LIGHTS DOWN, but a spotlight remains on TOILET SIGN.

On departure OFF, BOUNCER removes TOILET SIGN.

Moments pass … still no sign of CHLOE.

SOUND FX: Bell tinkle, more urgent.

LIGHTS down.

Scene 2.2 – It's Okay, I Washed It

LIGHTS up.

SOUND FX: Bell tinkles

Empty TABLE and CHAIR. Nothing happens.

CHLOE shouts from OFF.

CHLOE

Fuck!

CHLOE rushes ON with DRINK, cursing, then sits.

CHLOE

Sorry. I was in the toilet and didn't hear the bell.
I'm Chloe.

CHLOE offers hand to shake.

CHLOE

It's okay, I washed it. *(Shakes)*
Okay, behind schedule so … blah blah, happy,
friendly, sing and dance like nobody's watching.
(Thinks) Does anyone actually sing and dance
when on their own? Sounds nuts. Next, you're
asking your hat rack where it's going on holidays.
Are you into travelling? Brazil, Japan, Switzerland
– I've googled all of them. Be great to actually
go.

You're very quiet. What do you do for fun?

… Gaming? I am *so* shit at computer games. I once threw a Wii controller through a window. Though that might have been PMT.

… Oh. *Role-playing* gaming. So, people seriously still play Dungeons and Dragons? Like, adults with day jobs?

Well, that's sort of travelling. Exploring strange places, building experience, meeting people, then battering them to death with weaponry.

Sorry, I'm biased. I dated a D&D fanatic in high school. He was more interested in wrestling orcs than with me. The only ring he'd buy fired magic missiles at the undead.

All final year I waited to be asked to the Leaver's Ball. He took me to a Conan the Barbarian movie marathon instead. I fell asleep and choked on some popcorn. Luckily, the cinema usher knew first aid, so at least I got a snog.

He eventually dumped me. Crap D&D boyfriend, that is. The cinema usher preferred to focus on his film career. Seems I rated a poor second to make-believe.

Sadly, some of us roll low for charisma on the 20-sided dice of life.

SOUND FX: Bell tinkle.

CHLOE

You'd do so much better if you came out of your shell more. I'm better off going back into mine.

CHLOE covers her CARD but clearly writes a cross.

Confused, she picks up NOTE left by her "Opposite".

CHLOE

(*Reads*) "Don't put yourself down. I think you're beautiful."

CHLOE looks up but her "Opposite" has gone.

LIGHTS down.

Scene 2.3 – The Experienced Gentleman

SOUND FX: Bell tinkle.

LIGHTS up.

JACQUI sits at TABLE, much happier with circumstances.

JACQUI

Hello, I'm Jac- … (*Posh, mature voice*) Joanne.

She offers hand to shake, but her "Opposite" turns it and plants a gentlemanly kiss.

JACQUI

(*Very impressed*) Oh, charmed I'm sure, too, Charles. Lovely to see good old-fashioned manners, and dare I say *class* over on this side of proceedings. Whereas the hormone brigade over there, well, one doesn't want to imagine. There

comes a time when one needs a certain level of *maturity* in a partner. Someone who knows the important things in life. Knows quality. No sleeve tattoos.
… Oh, I don't drink, actually.
… Well, nothing alcoholic then.
… isn't that rather potent? I thought the top shelf was the harder liquors.
… Oh, they're up there for *smoothness* rather than alcohol content. Well, if I'll hardly notice it going down, why not? But a small one. With a mixer.
… isn't that alcoholic too?
… Really? I am learning things on this side of the room. But they don't have drinks waiters …

BOUNCER enters, unimpressed at being summoned by JACQUI's "Opposite".

JACQUI

Oh, with a snap of your fingers.

BOUNCER scowls, annoyed at this extension of duties, and departs OFF.

JACQUI

(Calls after BOUNCER) With lemonade. Confidence and class, that's what this side of the room has. So, what do you do, Charles?

JACQUI begins fanning herself with CARD.

JACQUI

Oh my. Quite the man of wealth and leisure.
Listen to me! Swooning like Scarlett O'Hara. It
must be your old-world charm and refinement.
… be my sugar daddy? Oh yes! Very *Gone With
the Wind*. Though I thought that was set on a
cotton plantation.

BOUNCER serves JACQUI a huge COCKTAIL with STRAW.

JACQUI

Oh, thank you.

*BOUNCER sternly places INVOICE on TABLE, then departs
OFF.*

JACQUI reacts in surprise to a tentative sip.

JACQUI

That's quite delicious actually. And absolutely no
alcohol?
… *Low* alcohol. Well, I suppose that's okay.
(Regards size of the glass) There *is* a lot here.
… I don't think there *is* any ice.

JACQUI takes a more adventurous sip.

JACQUI

I can taste the lemonade. Well, I think it's
lemonade. This could be the beginning of a
beautiful relationship indeed, Charles.

She toasts COCKTAIL with her "Opposite".

JACQUI

Frankly my dear, I *do* give a damn!

JACQUI takes another sip.

LIGHTS down.

Scene 2.4 – A New Leaf

SOUND FX: Bell tinkle.

LIGHTS up.

A more positive-minded TOM with PINT shakes hands with "Opposite".

TOM

Pleased to meet you, Amelia.
… Mixed night for me, but I realised I haven't
been giving it a decent go. So, that changes from
here on in. Completely fresh mindset.
… No. Nothing to do with my energy levels.
They're usually– …
… flower essences? No. I don't really– …
… No, I haven't considered homeopathic
remedies. Ever, actually.
… *(Winces)* Right.
… Is that so?

TOM glazes over as his "Opposite" continues.

TOM

And crystals. Really?
… Really.
… *Really?* Well, I guess that's why paramedics so
often turn to turquoise and lavender at accident
scenes.

TOM nods "cheers" then gulps from PINT.

LIGHTS down.

TOM remains at his TABLE for the next scene.

Scene 2.5 – Neg Hits

SOUND FX: Bell tinkle.

LIGHTS up.

MIKE enters, collar popped, strikes a pose.

He swaggers to TABLE, twists the CHAIR around and straddles it.

MIKE

Hey there, little lady.

He fist-bumps his "Opposite", then gives hand a little pained shake.

MIKE

Nice dress. You *nearly* fill it out quite well. A
friend of mine has one just like it.

… No, a female friend. And what would your name be?

… Well, *hello Deborah.*

They call me Mike. Rhymes with bike. Maybe you can ride me sometime.

… No, no training wheels. But you may need to hold tight – it could get *bumpy.*

… The planet I came down from? Probably the one you'll see lying on your back, gazing up at me and the stars.

… I don't think Uranus is visible to the human eye actually. So, what brings you here, little lady?

MIKE lazes back, hands behind head … and falls off CHAIR.

MIKE immediately resumes position astride CHAIR.

MIKE

Meant to do that. So, you like spontaneity in your men?

… No, I didn't run away to join any circuses. But keep it up, I like my women *feisty.*

MIKE makes whip-crack gesture and noise.

MIKE

You know, you have lovely eyes. A little crossed, but other than that, really lovely. Did you come along alone here tonight, or do you actually have friends?

… No, no. I came with my crew. My posse of bros. We're pretty tight. My wingman's just over there.

MIKE leans back and waves.

MIKE

Yo. Tom. My man.

MIKE makes warrior fist gesture.

At his TABLE, TOM gives the finger back at MIKE.

MIKE turns back, undaunted.

MIKE

That was my man. Tom.

… No, he was just indicating that I'm his number one man. Friend. Man-friend.

Yes, with that finger. It's a bro thing, you wouldn't understand. Don't worry your pretty little head about it.

So, do you work out? You *almost* have the figure to be a model.

… *(Flexes arms)* Yeah, I work out a lot.

… No, both arms. At the gym. Weights – heavy ones. Punching bag. That … elliptical walking thing.

… No, guys use them too. It's like cross country skiing. Do you ski? You look like you have a few challenging slopes under your belt. And a couple *above*, too.

… No, I haven't ever had my nose broken. I ski like a champ. It's all to do with hip motion.

MIKE makes suggestive hip rotations in CHAIR.

MIKE

… Of course I finished high school. So, how does a quite-pretty little thing like you happen to be single?
… *(Surprised)* Oh, and how long have you been lesbian?
… Three minutes? (Realises) Oh. Right.

MIKE turns his collar down, discouraged.

MIKE

Still … *(Pops collar back up)* If anyone can win you back to the other team, I'm your man.

LIGHTS immediately down.

SOUND FX: Drink splash to the face.

MIKE

At the very least, let me buy you a new drink.

MIKE exits OFF for costume change to a sodden SHIRT.

Scene 2.6 – Language Barrier

SOUND FX: Bell tinkle.

LIGHTS up.

At a new TABLE, JOANNE shakes hands with new "Opposite".

JOANNE

Nice to meet you, George. Well, here we are. We *young* ones. In *both* our primes.

The BOUNCER wanders past, checking JOANNE.

JOANNE proudly shows NAMETAG.

BOUNCER is suspicious, watching her all the way OFF.

SOUND FX: SMS arrives on JOANNE's MOBILE.

JOANNE pushes her MOBILE aside.

JOANNE

My name is Jacqui.
… ooh. *(Aping his exotic accent) Jacqui.* Very alluring accent you have there.
… *(Flattered, strokes hair)* Oh, thank you. You're quite the complimenter. *(Giggles)* Oh, shush.
(Flirty) Very alluring accent. So, what do you do, George?
… "You look for the new wife". Well, that can take up a lot of free time.
… I'm sure you do "Be look very hard". And what else do you do besides wife-hunting?
… Tennis and squash. Great.
… Yes, I like tennis and squash also.
… And your pencil is red. Okay...
… Yes, it does sound like you're "new person to country".

… No, we've had tennis and squash here for
quite some time now.

JOANNE is startled by "Opposite" grasping her hands.

JOANNE

Oh, we're holding hands already.
… You actually mentioned my lovely eyes before.
… And my lovely hair.
… *(Frowns)* It's not really the time for tennis or
squash just now.
… No, I'm not a wife at the moment.

JOANNE politely laughs, withdrawing hands.

JOANNE

But the night is young. You might meet lots of
wives yet.
… Yes, and play tennis with them.
… "You give me the compliments again". Okay.
Sure.

*JOANNE responds with a range of facial reactions to a string of
bizarre compliments, finally settling on "bewildered".*

JOANNE

Right… Thank you. Very poetic. A bit abstract.
You did paint yourself into a corner trying to
rhyme "mongoose".

JOANNE grows disenchanted.

JOANNE

You've already said my eyes are lovely.
… And my hair. *(Touches hair, confused)* "Is thick
and healthy"?
Oh! *Your* hair is "thick and healthy". Fair enough.
… Not your hair?
… oh right. *That's* thick and healthy too. *(Sighs)*
And you were doing so well, George.

SOUND FX: SMS arrives on JOANNE's MOBILE.

JOANNE rolls her eyes and checks MOBILE.

JOANNE

(Peers) Hang on, that's a new one.

She arches an eyebrow at "Opposite".

JOANNE

If I find out this is yours, George, you're in *such*
big trouble.

LIGHTS down.

Scene 2.7 – Jockeys

LIGHTS up.

CHLOE is midway through a session at a different TABLE.

CHLOE

A friend of mine had this run of jockeys approaching her on online dating. Apparently if you don't specify a preferred height in a partner, then *voom*! They're in there, jockeys climbing over themselves to try their luck. Not that I'm heightist or anything. I've never even considered the height thing before. I mean, who cares? But … *jockeys*. Where do you draw the line?
(Holds hand to side) About here, according to my friend.

Because it wasn't just an occasional one. This was like, *heaps* of them. You start to wonder if you're giving off some sort of horsey vibe. "What's with all the fucking jockeys?" My friend said. So, I'd pour her another wine and try to calm her down. We had a *lot* of wine for a while there.

So, I said, maybe give it a go. On a date. Who knows, might be great. Leave the "logistics" till later if things work out. But the guy she picked – what an arsehole. Arrogant, dismissed her opinions, rude to their waiter. So, she called him out, said he had a Napoleon Complex. That *really* did not go down well.

Eventually, she had to write "No Jockeys" on her dating profile, just to put a stop to it all. Then she got this flood of angry messages accusing her of being heightist. She ended up *banned* from the site. Bloody jockeys.

So, she started hanging around basketball matches instead. Met this point guard. She barely came up to his armpits. But they found a way of making it work, once he changed deodorant.

She could sort of see their perspective then, the jockeys. It got me thinking about dating. Mostly that there's a lot of jockeys out there, looking for love. Looking for some way to make it work out. Just like the rest of us.

I really hope they find it one day.

LIGHTS up on TOM at a TABLE.

TOM

I dunno, it does make you sound *pretty* heightist.

CHLOE

Does it? *(Deflates)* Bugger.

SOUND FX: Bell rings.

LIGHTS down.

Scene 2.8 – Now, That's Funny

LIGHTS UP.

Two empty COCKTAILS sit on TABLE with JACQUI now exuberantly tipsy with broad hand gestures.

She leans forward, pointing a belligerent but swaying finger.

JACQUI

Hey. Hey! I know all about having fun, thanks, buster. I have watched the movie Zoolander over *twenty* times.

JACQUI authoratively holds up random fingers.

JACQUI

So I've a *pretty* good idea what fun is, thank you very much.

BOUNCER delivers another COCKTAIL. JACQUI throws her arms in celebration.

JACQUI

Hurray!

She immediately stands, looking about the room.

JACQUI

Charles? *(Waves)* Charles! Yoo hoo! Thank you, Charles! You're a prince!

She blows a huge air kiss, then flops back into CHAIR.

She notices her "Opposite" with disappointment.

JACQUI

Oh, it's you again.

She frowns then realises something.

JACQUI

Ha! Prince Charles.

She finds herself terribly amusing with a drunken snorting laugh.

JACQUI

That "fun" enough for ya, grandpa?

LIGHTS down.

Scene 2.9 – The Pilot Episode

LIGHTS up.

His SHIRT noticeably sodden, MIKE is struggling at a new TABLE.

MIKE

So, what do you do for a living, he said, resorting to most boring question ever.

He receives a most surprising answer.

MIKE

Oh! You're a … really? Right. Okay. Well, that's different. And very honest of you, being comfortable about … that. And why shouldn't you be, you wouldn't get too far in that profession by being shy and retiring.
So, business been good lately? Obviously not asking for a blow-by-blow job description- … asking for *work details* or anything.

… Rushed off your feet? Right. Though, in your line, you're not on your feet most of the time, are you? Will you be going off for a shift after we finish up here?

… No, fair enough too. All work and no play, you'd be buggered- … Jiggered- … Rooted- … *Tired!* Tired.

So how did you get into that line of work? Were you sort of hard up for cash?

… A training course? I'd have thought it was more learn as you went, *"On the job"*.

… Complete a logbook? What, of names and positions?

… Flying hours? Like, in a plane?

… Oh! You said *pilot!* Sorry! I completely misheard. I thought you said *harlot*. That makes *so* much more sense now. Sorry. I'm not good with accents, and yours is quite thick. Not unintelligible. Just heavy, and I don't have an ear for South African.

… New Zealand, really? Well, they are quite similar.

… Okay, not very similar. I just misheard pilot for … that other line of work. Which I most definitely couldn't see you doing. Not that I'm saying you *couldn't* make a living that way. You're *very* attractive so could probably make a fortune if you were to put your … *mind* to it. Not that I'm visualising you doing it or anything. Just saying that you easily *could,* for money, and do really very well indeed.

Maybe even more than you do as a pilot.

… Why do you need to call security?

MIKE watches "Opposite" walk away.

SOUND FX: A pencil drops on the floor.

MIKE instantly looks round but can't see CHLOE.

He notices his "Opposite" returning.

MIKE

Oh, you're back. I hope I didn't-

LIGHTS immediately down.

SOUND FX: Drink splash to the face.

MIKE exits OFF for costume change to even wetter drink-stained SHIRT.

Scene 2.10 – Vice Males

SOUND FX: SMS Received on JOANNE's MOBILE.

JOANNE

Fuck. Off!

Scene 2.11 – Ex's and Selfies

LIGHTS up.

TOM sits awkwardly at TABLE, "Opposite" sitting on his jutted knee.

He is forcing a smile as "Opposite" takes a selfie.

TOM

Surely three selfies are enough?

Relieved, he assists "Opposite" off his lap to return to her side of TABLE.

TOM

No, don't tag me.
You're posting all of those?
… one with every guy tonight?
… Yeah, that should make your ex annoyed and jealous. But how do you know he's keeping watch on you?
… Because you're keeping watch on him. And you don't think he's posting flirty pictures too?
… Yeah, they probably are all scrags.
… No, I switched off my social media. The whole "official" defriending thing seemed a bit high-school-drama. Easier to just deactivate and disappear.
… Actually, I can live with the lost friend counts. I prefer not to torture myself with unexpected updates and pictures. Who they're talking to, who they're adding. How quickly they respond to certain peoples' postings. How quickly those certain people post back.
"There lies madness."
Better to go do some real stuff, try some new fun things. *(Sighs) Or,* go speed dating.

… Three likes for our picture already? Wow …

TOM is alarmed as "Opposite" rush around to him again.

TOM

No. Another selfie would really be overdoing it.
Less is more.

TOM reacts as "Opposite" barges onto his lap.

He holds his head back, hovering his arm.

TOM

Your breasts are sort of in my face– …
No, no. It's much funnier if I look straight ahead.
(Reacts) Whoah! No wiggling.

TOM forces a smile, eyes not wavering.

"Opposite" leaps off his lap and returns to her side of TABLE.

TOM

Yep, he sure will go nuts about that one.
You don't think it's a bit desperate though?
Needing to be validated by his jealousy?
… Me turning off my social media is hardly the
same. I didn't care if she noticed that I
disappeared. I can't see her activities, she can't see
mine. What I don't know can't hurt me. What I
knew already, already had.
She's met someone else anyway. Almost straight
away as it happens. *After*, I presume. Maybe

before. I try not to think too much about it. Try, anyway.

… Exactly. "There lies madness."

SOUND FX: Bell tinkles.

TOM

Fifteen likes already? Wow …

LIGHTS down.

Scene 2.12 – Mr Andrews

LIGHTS up.

JACQUI sips COCKTAIL, now very squiffy indeed.

She squints at newly arrived "Opposite" then recognises him.

JACQUI

Mr Andrews? It *is* you, isn't it! You taught me maths in high school.
You did! You called me "Jacqui the Robot" because I *always* answered first. *(Recollects)* So did the other kids, the shitheads. I haven't seen you for *years* and *years* and *years*. And *years*! Is Mrs Andrews here too?
… She left you? Awwww.
… Aha! We *all* knew there was something going on with Mr Kenny! They were on playground duty together a bit *too* often for chance. Slipping off to his PE shed to *(Air quotes)* "inflate the

sport equipment". *So* obvious! Well, except to you.

Mr Kenny, eh? What an arsehole. All the other girls had a crush on him. All muscley under his tight shirts, and those short little shorts he wore every day.

… you okay?

(Lifts drink) You should have one of these. *Non-*alcoholic. Here, smell.

JACQUI waves COCKTAIL in vicinity of "Opposite's" nose.

JACQUI

See, not a whiffybird. This is my third. Fourth. Third. Whatever. Still …

JACQUI leans forward to give "Opposite's" shoulder a haphazard hearty pat.

JACQUI

Good on you. Good. On. *You*! Getting out here, looking for someone new. Did you go to the school reunion?

… yeah, s'pose they would've been there. Next one maybe?

… No, I guess the pain never will go away.

Me? I'm doing shit hot. Got a great job. No one calls me Jacqui the Robot there! Not since I sent that office email. No partner though. That's why I'm here, looking for someone to "make my grade".

… You already gave me a grade, years ago.

… Well, yeah, we are both adults now.

… *(Frowns)* I don't think that would be very appropriate, Mr Andrews. Besides, my uniform wouldn't even fit anymore. *Really*, Mr Andrews, you've *so* gone out of my top ten teachers.
… No, Mr Kenny wasn't in my top ten.
… No, I wouldn't say yes if Mr Kenny asked. *(Peers forward)* Are you crying, Mr Andrews?
… Yes, it is smoky in here. Probably very unhealthy for all of us.
… Yes, Mr Kenny was *very* fit and healthy.

JACQUI pokes COCKTAIL with STRAW.

JACQUI

You really should try one of these drinks, Mr Andrews.
… Mr Andrews?

JACQUI peers forward.

JACQUI

Ah! You *are* crying, aren't you.

SOUND FX: Bell tinkles.

Scene 2.13 – Ethical Non-Monogamy

JACQUI slowly rises then staggers to next TABLE, while …

… MIKE enters in an even more soiled SHIRT. He sits at TABLE as his new "Opposite" comments.

MIKE

No, not a nervous sweater. I just mistook
someone for being a hooker.
… Yeah, that's what she said.

… JOANNE enters, fingers crossed, muttering a mantra.

JOANNE

Please no crap beard. Please no crap beard. Please
no crap beard.

JOANNE sits at a TABLE, waiting for her "Opposite" to arrive.

*… TOM enters with PINT, sits at a TABLE, nods greeting to
"Opposite".*

TOM

Once more unto the breach.

*… as CHLOE enters and sits at a TABLE, summoning her
confidence.*

CHLOE

Hey, I'm Chloe. Please be normal.

NOTE: MIKE and CHLOE never meet/ sit at adjacent tables.

*… as JACQUI finally reaches remaining CHAIR. She leans heavily
on it, distinctly, but waves away offers of assistance.*

JACQUI

I got this.

JACQUI proceeds to slowly sit as dialogue continues.

JOANNE's "Opposite" has arrived.

JOANNE

(Masking pain) That's quite an impressive beard you have.

MIKE

Otherwise, my night has been going great.

CHLOE

Really great night.

TOM

(Uninterested) Oh, great. *(Drinks)*

JOANNE points to her "Opposite's" chin.

JOANNE

Actually, you have some crumbs … *(Points elsewhere)* And there.

CHLOE

Though there have been a few weirdos.

JOANNE

(Points elsewhere) And just along- … Look, who the fuck are you, the Cookie Monster?

MIKE

No, no tattoos. Though you've got quite a few. I quite like that one- *(Instant recoil)* Ooh, no I don't.

… Rough childhood?

TOM

No, my resting face is often mistaken for abject boredom.

SOUND FX: SMS arrives on JOANNE's MOBILE.

JOANNE

(Gritted teeth) Just ignore it.

CHLOE

Unless everyone else is normal and I'm the weird one!

CHLOE snorts a laugh, then instantly covers mouth in alarm.

JACQUI waves away offers of assistance …

JACQUI

I got this.

… but doesn't proceed much further.

JOANNE

You're into "Ethical Non-Monogamy"? Is that like a Swingers Party with a low carbon footprint?

CHLOE

You seem really nice, though.

TOM

No, go on. I'm *absolutely* fascinated.

MIKE

Not much luck tonight so far. You?

CHLOE

I'm too wimpy to get a body piercing.

JOANNE

So, multiple relationships with all partners' consent?

MIKE

Go home with you – in your ute …?

CHLOE

So, where is this piercing of yours?

JACQUI

(Stop hand-signal) I got this.

JOANNE

Polyamory sounds an awful lot like just rootin' around.

MIKE

How far out of town is your farm?

CHLOE

Not your eyebrows, obviously.

TOM

(Stop hand-signal) Hang on. I'm not *quite* drunk enough to make it to the end of your story.

TOM embarks on a guzzle, stop hand-signal remaining up ...

JOANNE

And your partner is fine with you here picking up tonight?

MIKE

You *would* let me go afterwards?

CHLOE

Nipples?

JOANNE

(Raises MOBILE) Shall we call her about that?

CHLOE

(Squints, deducing) Not in your tongue.

JOANNE

Okay, and we'll call him as well.

MIKE

No, I don't want to arm wrestle you for it.

CHLOE

Surely not your *old fella*!

JOANNE

How many partners do you have?

JACQUI

(Stop hand-signal) I got this.

JOANNE

I'd be happy just to find one.

CHLOE

I give up. Where is this piercing then?

MIKE assumes arm wrestling position with his "Opposite".

MIKE

Wow, you've got really callused hands.

CHLOE

No! Say it ain't the taint.

JOANNE

They say you can meet someone at the
supermarket checkout.

CHLOE

I did notice you sat down very carefully.

MIKE's arm collapses onto TABLE, vanquished.

MIKE

(Fearful) ... Best of five?

... finally, TOM comes up for air, lowers PINT and hand.

TOM

Okay, this dream you had … Pray, go on.

MIKE

Why would I need a safe word?
… Oh.
Can I use it now?

CHLOE

Funnily enough, the word "perineum" won me school spelling champion.

TOM

Maybe it symbolises that you're quite tedious?

JOANNE

I mostly use the self-serve nowadays. A few swishes and I'm done.

TOM

A pinch on the arm can sometimes wake you from a horrible dream. *(Pinches his arm)* Nope, I'm still here.

MIKE

I'd just prefer someone a little less … Wolf Creek-y.

JOANNE

I am *not* running out of time!

SOUND FX: Bell tinkles

… just as JACQUI finally plonks down in CHAIR.

JACQUI

For fuck's sake. *(Slumps onto TABLE)*

MIKE instantly stands.

MIKE

Bugger, out of time. Bye!

MIKE looks for his next table, while …

… TOM innocently shrugs, then rises laboriously ….

… as CHLOE offers to shake, then withdraws and waves instead as she leaves.

JOANNE, CHLOE, TOM and MIKE move to their next TABLE.

NOTE: MIKE and CHLOE move so as not to encounter each other.

TOM

(Weary) How many more rounds to go?

BOUNCER enters, holding NUMBERED CARD "5".

TOM

I don't think I'll make it.

BOUNCER reveals PINT in other hand.

TOM *takes it, crisis averted, then sits at his next TABLE.*

MIKE

Hi, Naomi.

CHLOE

(Writing name) Nick.

TOM

Hey Stephanie.

JOANNE

Your parents didn't seriously name you *Zephyr*.

JACQUI grunts and flicks her hand as though someone has tapped her arm.

CHLOE

C, H, L, O, E.
… Meh. "Chloe-sy" enough. Fuck, did I just say that?

MIKE

I wouldn't say *totally* disastrous.

TOM

I would.

JACQUI sits up as though nudged awake.

JACQUI

Who are you?

MIKE

I'm having a great night.

JOANNE

Are you stoned?

CHLOE

Well, I do have a lot of Adele on my playlist.

TOM

I'm really not interested tonight to be honest.

SOUND FX: SMS arrives on JOANNE's MOBILE.

JOANNE

Just ignore that.

JACQUI

(Dragging hand over face) Jacqui, with four N's and a quack for all I care.

CHLOE

You're a DJ? Cool!

MIKE

I can never find anyone to play with.

TOM

No, no, I wasn't issuing a challenge.

CHLOE

Play at any nightclubs I might go to?

MIKE

I spent my teens banging it out against a wall.

CHLOE

As if I go to nightclubs anymore.

JOANNE

How did you get it through Customs?

TOM is surprised by something under TABLE.

TOM

Is that your foot? *(Freezes)* Whoah!

TOM sits rigid as "Opposite" plays very naughty "footsies".

JACQUI

(Squints in suspicion) Is that a toupee?

MIKE

So, I thought, "Why not make it a foursome?"

JOANNE

I wouldn't have thought to look there either.

JACQUI

(Points) There! It moved again.

CHLOE

Do they go much on doof-doof at RSLs?

JOANNE

Well, that's airport security for you. Very thorough.

TOM is still wide-eyed by the "footsies" below.

TOM

Yep, I *am* impressed. That zip's been stuck for weeks.

MIKE

A few too many off the wrist for my liking.

CHLOE

(Losing interest) You DJ weddings as well?

JOANNE

So, who raised your bail?

TOM's facial expressions can only hint at what's happening beneath TABLE.

TOM

Who knew bunions could be so useful.

JACQUI

And I have suspicions about your moustache too.

MIKE

I generally prefer a forehand grip.

JOANNE

I'm going to ask you to stop talking now.

MIKE

We *are* still talking about tennis, aren't we?

JOANNE

No, really. Sssh.

CHLOE

(Very unsure now) Do funerals often need a DJ?

The novelty worn off, TOM is less impressed by "Opposite's" attentions.

TOM

You know, this isn't quite as erotic as adult films suggest.

SOUND FX: Bell tinkle

JACQUI

Telephone!

TOM is concerned – his "Opposite" has left him with a "predicament" below.

BOUNCER walks in with a "4" NUMBERED CARD.

MIKE, CHLOE, and JOANNE switch TABLES.

MIKE hovers at TOM's TABLE, waiting for him to move.

JACQUI gives her departing "Opposite" the "I'm watching you" signal.

TOM stands carefully, holding PINT and SCORECARD at crotch level, then discreetly sidesteps to next available TABLE.

MIKE gives the TABLE a little check before sitting.

CHLOE

Chloe.

JOANNE

Joanne.

TOM

Tom.

MIKE

Mike

JACQUI

(Resting head on folded arms) Jesus.

MIKE

Yeah, everyone says I look nervous.

CHLOE

It wouldn't be my photo you saw. I haven't online dated for *years.* … Months.

MIKE

Mostly because I generally am very nervous.

JOANNE is stroking her new "Opposite's" beard.

JOANNE

(Deflated) Yes, that is the softest beard I've ever felt.

JACQUI

(With talking hand) Talk talk. Blah blah.

CHLOE

Okay, it was my photo. Did you swipe left or right?

TOM

I'm reasonably financially secure, I guess.

CHLOE

(Disappointed) Ah. Left.

JOANNE

Are you speaking in emoji?

SOUND FX: SMS arrives on JOANNE's MOBILE.

JACQUI

Telephone!

JOANNE

(Grimacing) Just ignore that.

TOM

Sure, I'm interested in promising investment returns.

MIKE

I tried meditating. With a phone app. I got up to *level* 5!

CHLOE

Well, I thought it was a nice photo.

JACQUI

Doesn't matter. I'm already promised to a *complete gentleman.*

MIKE

What, meditate *now?*

JOANNE

My evening? Slightly penis-heavy.

TOM

A once in a lifetime opportunity for my friends and family too?

JACQUI

He *is* a gentleman. *Four* drinks he's bought me. *(Shows random fingers)*

CHLOE

I was once dumped for using full stops in my messages.

MIKE reacts as "Opposite" clasps his hands.

MIKE

Ooh, cold hands!

MIKE *closes his eyes, self-consciously joining his "Opposite" in hand-held meditation.*

JACQUI

Non-alcoholic, actually.

CHLOE

Apparently full stops signify anger or insincerity.

JOANNE

… Towards the end of my thirties.

BOUNCER *delivers another COCKTAIL to JACQUI.*

JACQUI

Five drinks.

CHLOE

Isn't it hard enough without being judged on punctuation as well?

JACQUI stands to wave somewhere in distance.

JACQUI

Thank you, Charles! *(Huge air kiss)* Mmmmwhah!

BOUNCER *frowns in concern. JACQUI frowns back, sitting.*

MIKE

You *are* chanting your "Omms" *quite* loudly.

TOM

Are you trying to sign me up to a pyramid investment scheme?

JOANNE

Never married. By choice. Mine, not theirs.

CHLOE leans forward, menacing with her PEN.

CHLOE

Mind you, … use more than one exclamation mark at a time, and I will gut you like a pig.

TOM picks up BROCHURE from his TABLE.

TOM

You've brought brochures?

CHLOE

(Sits back, cheery) Nah, not really.

JOANNE

Not weird. Just choosy.

CHLOE

(Forward, threatening with PEN) Actually, no. *Really.*

TOM

That's a different shape, but still *quite* pyramid-y.

MIKE

The only thing I feel mindful of is people looking at us.

JOANNE

I wouldn't call them bad choices.

TOM

What my occupation? I'm a tax office inspector.

TOM's "Opposite" immediately scampers away.

TOM

(Quickly) Yeah okay seeya bye.

Pleased with his work, TOM sits back and reads BROCHURE.

CHLOE

So, why is this friend of yours still single?

MIKE frees his hands from "Opposite's" clasp.

MIKE

Well, that was certainly quite an experience.

CHLOE

(Disappointed) He's a jockey. What are the odds of that?

TOM

(Reading BROCHURE) Actually, that's quite a good return.

JOANNE

Independent and self-sufficient, not "sad and lonely".

MIKE waves hand across "Opposite's" face – she is in a trance.

MIKE

… hello?

SOUND FX: Bell tinkle

JACQUI

Telephone!

MIKE

Hello?

JOANNE

Goodbye.

TOM, CHLOE and JOANNE get up and look for next TABLES. JACQUI remains seated, feeling queasy.

MIKE taps his "Opposite" on the shoulder, then quietly moves away, leaving her in a trance.

TOM hands BROCHURE to MIKE in passing, then all sit at TABLES.

BOUNCER walks in holding up a "3" NUMBERED CARD.

MIKE

Umm, Pisces.

CHLOE

Sagittarius.

TOM

Pyrex.

JOANNE

I think I'm a Libra.

JACQUI

I think I'm going to be sick.

CHLOE

Coffee.

JOANNE

Dinner.

MIKE

Probably the movies?

CHLOE

Not on the first date.

JACQUI

That was one of my questions!

TOM

I don't *do* dating at the moment.

MIKE

So, what do you do then?

CHLOE

Maybe a snog?

JOANNE

McDonald's *does not* count as a dinner date.

JACQUI

I *should* have someone already.

TOM

I will when I'm ready.

JACQUI

Big freakin' mystery to me too.

JOANNE

Smashed avocado?

CHLOE

I dunno, I'm easy.

MIKE

I wish it *was* easier.

CHLOE

Not *that* easy.

JACQUI

I have *an office* of my own at work.

TOM

I don't still have a flame burning.

JACQUI

No one else has an office.

JOANNE

(*Guilty admission*) Okay, Forty … ish.

JACQUI

Just me. Alone.

TOM

Any flame is out. Snuffed.

MIKE

Maybe tonight. Maybe you.

CHLOE

Maybe?

MIKE

Okay, maybe not.

JACQUI

My life is under *complete* control.

TOM

And I have the burn marks to prove it.

JACQUI

Someone of similar quality.

MIKE

Something has to work eventually.

CHLOE

I'm beginning to doubt it.

JACQUI

Who can take adequate direction.

JOANNE

I don't have any regrets.

TOM

I'm *not* stuck on regrets.

JOANNE

Except Simon. He was a huge mistake.

CHLOE

Maybe for some, there isn't a good fit.

MIKE

If not tonight there's always next time.

JACQUI

(Emphatic) I want to be wooed!

MIKE

Or the time after that.

JOANNE

But we don't have our time over again.

CHLOE

Maybe for some of us, there is no "one".

TOM

I have moved on. Way on.

JACQUI

Wooed by suitors to choose from.

CHLOE

Maybe some of us are just "one-offs".

JOANNE

It's onwards, for better or worse.

JACQUI

I'll know love when I see it, buster.

TOM

I'm as open as I want to be.

JACQUI

I'd like to see love.

TOM

And as closed as I need to be.

JOANNE

Or worse or worser, it increasingly seems.

JACQUI

Just for once.

CHLOE

Sometimes I worry I won't make anyone's grade.

MIKE

I think she's still here somewhere.

JOANNE

Just a little hope occasionally would be nice.

CHLOE

I never seem to make anyone's grade.

JOANNE

Just occasionally.

JACQUI morosely sings, sufficiently off-key from any legally recognisable song.

JACQUI

"Where-ere-ere is my love?"

SOUND FX: SMS arrives on JOANNE's MOBILE.

JOANNE

(Shouts at MOBILE) Fuck! Off!

Everyone else looks in random directions (but not directly at JOANNE) to where the shout has come from, relative to their location.

Aware the entire venue is looking at her, JOANNE places her MOBILE aside.

JOANNE

Telemarketer.

Everyone reverts attention to their "Opposites".

JACQUI

(Wearily slaps TABLE) I'm done.

JACQUI haughtily struts OFF in haphazard, fashion.

JOANNE

So, look what you have to look forward to.

MIKE

Maybe I am trying too hard.

CHLOE

That *possibly* came across as a bit needy.

TOM

I guess we agree to disagree then.

MIKE

But it is hard for some of us.

JOANNE

Never know, you might be luckier.

CHLOE

Let's talk about funny internet cat videos instead.

JOANNE

Maybe I'm just you with years on.

TOM

I am … getting another drink.

TOM departs OFF with empty PINT.

JOANNE

Some microwave dinners-for-one are quite edible.

CHLOE

Dog videos then?

MIKE

(Checking shirt) Does rum and coke stain?

JOANNE

I doubt I *could* share a tv remote now.

MIKE

I bought this shirt especially for tonight.

CHLOE

Meerkats?

JOANNE

My couch fits just me, just right.

CHLOE

Actually, I need to go to the toilet.

CHLOE quickly departs OFF.

MIKE

They say love comes when you're not looking.

JOANNE

Maybe I'm just tired of looking.

MIKE

But won't I just look disinterested?

JOANNE

I'm not going to settle for whoever's closest.

MIKE

A bit the way you look now.

JOANNE

Near enough, good enough?

MIKE

Sorry.

JOANNE

Near enough is not even close.

MIKE

Ha, try being myself?

JOANNE

And if that means, for now no one, then so be it.

MIKE

But I *am* just being myself.

SOUND FX: Bell tinkles.

MIKE

That's the problem.

LIGHTS DOWN

Scene 2.14 – Message Filters

LIGHTS up.

BOUNCER crosses stage with a "2" NUMBERED CARD. A TABLE may be removed while passing through.

JOANNE and TOM sit at their respective TABLES.

TOM

Hi Jacqui.

JOANNE

Actually, I'm Joanne.

TOM

Your nametag says Jacqui.

JOANNE

A few people have been confused by that.

TOM

Probably because your nametag says Jacqui.

JOANNE

Which I've since crossed out and written Joanne. See?

TOM

(Squinting) In very faint pencil.

JOANNE

I only had a pencil.

TOM

Though not when you wrote "Jacqui" in big black marker.

JOANNE

I had things on my mind at the time.

TOM

Someone called Jacqui presumably.

JOANNE

Yes. Another person entirely.

TOM

Person, or *personality*?

JOANNE

I'm not sure Jacqui actually has a personality.

TOM

Or her nametag.

JOANNE

She has mine.

JOANNE ducks as BOUNCER walks past behind TOM.

TOM looks round to see BOUNCER departing, removing another TABLE if required.

TOM

Are you on the run from the police?

JOANNE

No, just security.

SOUND FX: SMS arrives on JOANNE's MOBILE.

They "look" to her MOBILE. JOANNE ignores it as best she can.

JOANNE

Any idea why we're subjecting ourselves to all
this?

TOM

Crap conniving friends. You?

JOANNE

Masochism. Self-inflicted.

TOM

Any luck so far?

JOANNE

Really bad. You?

TOM

I've taken to drinking heavily.

JOANNE

I may join you.

A moment's realisation – are they flirting?

SOUND FX: SMS arrives on JOANNE's MOBILE.

TOM

You can check those if you want.

JOANNE

No, I don't need or want to.

TOM

Ignoring someone?

JOANNE

As much as I can. Long story. Short on time.

SOUND FX: SMS arrives on JOANNE's MOBILE.

TOM

They're pretty insistent.

JOANNE

They're *incredibly* insistent.

TOM

Block the number.

JOANNE

It's more than one. Possibly an entire football team.

TOM

… okay.

JOANNE

I think one had a tattoo of the team mascot. They won't stop messaging.

TOM

Arseholes.

JOANNE

Not as yet but give them time.

SOUND FX: SMS arrives on JOANNE's MOBILE.

JOANNE

I'll have to change my phone number.

TOM

Have you tried telling them to fuck off?

JOANNE

Have you not heard me yelling?

TOM

I thought that was some drunk. *(Holds out hand)*
Let me try.

JOANNE pulls MOBILE to herself protectively.

JOANNE

You don't know what sort of messages they are.

TOM

I think I've been around a bit.

JOANNE hesitantly passes MOBILE across TABLE (and out of sight).

TOM picks up identical MOBILE from his TABLE, recoils from the picture.

TOM

Holy cripes almighty!

TOM pushes MOBILE away onto TABLE (and out of sight).

JOANNE snatches up MOBILE from her TABLE.

JOANNE

I did warn you.

TOM

You didn't say anything about blinding me with cock!

JOANNE

I thought you'd "been around a bit".

TOM

Not around other guys' penises.

JOANNE

We women are expected to deal with them all the time.

TOM

Do you normally show dick pics to guys you've just met?

JOANNE

I'm not showing dick pics. Well, I am but they're not mine. Jesus, Tom, show a bit of backbone. Harden up.

TOM looks up in surprise.

JOANNE

Figuratively speaking!

TOM

I think my retinas are burnt.

JOANNE

Great, the only vaguely tickable guy all night and I sexually harass him.

TOM

Only *vaguely* tickable?

JOANNE

Compared to everyone else so far. Two minutes in and you haven't shown me your genitalia. I'm calling that a win. *(Wary)* You're not, are you?

TOM

I wasn't intending to.

JOANNE

Good.

TOM

Are all of them just pictures?

JOANNE

(Nods) Typing probably requires both hands.

TOM

Then we can filter out multimedia attachments. Call it a cock block.

SOUND FX: SMS arrives on JOANNE's MOBILE.

JOANNE instinctively looks at MOBILE, recoils, then looks again.

JOANNE

It *is* a tattoo. … Can I trust you?

TOM

Only trying to help.

JOANNE warily places MOBILE on TABLE.

JOANNE

Promise you won't take pictures of your penis?

TOM

I should be able to contain myself.

JOANNE pushes MOBILE forward (and out of sight).

TOM picks up identical MOBILE from his TABLE. He squeamishly navigates, not wanting to touch the pictures.

TOM

Wow, what a bunch of pricks.

JOANNE

Why do guys do it? Is it some fifteen centimetres of fame thing?

TOM

(Swishing on MOBILE) Here we go. Filter options.

JOANNE

When did you learn to number block?

TOM

I had to set one up recently.

JOANNE

Too many incoming calls?

TOM

Too many outgoing.

JOANNE nods in sympathy – she's been there too.

TOM

Done.

TOM pushes MOBILE along TABLE (and out of sight).

JOANNE picks up MOBILE from her TABLE.

TOM

I think I need hand sanitiser.

JOANNE

And this will stop them coming … so to speak.

TOM

Any new ones. I'll let you "dispose" of what's already there. Just remove the block when you change phone numbers.

JOANNE

Have you removed yours?

TOM isn't able to answer, when …

SOUND FX: Bell tinkle.

JOANNE

Shit, we barely started.

TOM

And with the only vaguely tickable girl all night.

They smile, TOM stands and pushes in CHAIR.

JOANNE

(Blurts) I'm over forty.

TOM is surprised by the outburst, but shrugs.

TOM

You don't look it.

JOANNE

… You don't have a score card.

TOM

I'm not here to meet anyone. Long story. Short on time.

JOANNE

(Holds MOBILE) … Thanks for the phone.

TOM

Thanks for the blinding flash.

LIGHTS down.

TOM and JOANNE depart OFF.

Scene 2.15 – Jacqui's Last Stand

LIGHTS slowly fade up.

JACQUI is standing on TABLE, sway-dancing, slowly undoing her blouse.

JACQUI

(Slurred singing) Who wants to see my … *boobies?*
Who wants to see my pretty boobies?

BOUNCER strides up to her and crosses arms, unimpressed.

JACQUI notices BOUNCER, then gives jazz hands.

JACQUI

Boobies!

JOANNE dashes ON, stares in horror then mouths "Fuck".

LIGHTS down as JOANNE helps JACQUI down and OFF.

BOUNCER may take another TABLE OFF.

Scene 2.16 – Haven't We Met Before?

LIGHTS up.

MIKE enters and sits at same TABLE as the opening scene, as …

… BOUNCER crosses stage with a "1" NUMBERED CARD. Another TABLE may be taken OFF.

MIKE

Hi. *(Frowns)* Haven't we met before? At one of these nights, months ago. I thought so! You were into rock climbing. We were matched afterwards. I sent you an email. Straight away.

You didn't reply.

… yeah, probably the spam filter. Though I didn't say anything in it like "cheap Viagra for sale". Even the email servers are out to spoil my love life.

Then I could hardly send a second one. "Hi, just emailing again in case you somehow missed the first, unless of course you were totally rejecting me. Awkward!"

Bit disappointing really. Actually getting a match, summoning the courage to contact, and then … nothing. We might have really hit it off six months ago.

… You had seven matches that night? Wow, no wonder you didn't need to repl- … receive my email.

Of course, I was busy sorting through all *my* matches. Some good potential possibilities.

… Well, obviously I'm back here tonight. Obviously the same for you. Seven dead ends. I might've been your eighth. And how often do second chance speed dates come along? Ships passing on *another* night.

Though, only if you tick me again. And I tick you, of course. No guarantees, young lady!

Maybe my email will get through this time. Or we could just exchange numbers now?

… Sure, we should follow the proper process. That's what I do, too. Be warned, though – I'm gathering quite a few ticks tonight myself. One girl in particular, we had quite a connection.

SOUND FX: Pencil drops on floor.

MIKE instantly looks around but sees no sign of CHLOE.

He returns to his "Opposite" with a weak smile.

MIKE

Second chances, eh? Though imagine how embarrassing it would be, bumping into someone you matched last time and then they just totally crossed you out. Imagine how terrible that would feel.

SOUND FX: Bell tinkle.

Mike's smile fades.

MIKE

Like you're going to do now.

MIKE watches "Opposite" depart.

MIKE

Yeah. Those damn spam filters.

MIKE looks at his CARD but doesn't mark a score.

Scene 2.17 – And It's Over

SOUND FX: General bar chatter grows louder.

MIKE stands then walks forward to mingle with the "Crowd".

He casts a tired look. Too many nights have ended like this.

An "Opposite" approaches him.

MIKE

Oh hi.
… Yeah, it does looks like it will probably kick
on.
… Another free Cosmo?
… No, I don't think I'll stay. I've got a … thing to
go to. A couch, to be honest. I just came for the
speed dating really.

*BOUNCER enters with decorated SCOREBOX labelled "SCORE!
BOX" with slot in the top.*

BOUNCER holds SCOREBOX out for MIKE.

MIKE looks at his CARD, then tears it up and departs OFF.

BOUNCER shrugs, then places SCOREBOX on TABLE.

*BOUNCER re-sets TOILET sign on the wall then departs, taking
CHAIRS if required.*

CHLOE enters from "TOILET" to stand self-consciously with COCKTAIL and CARD. She fails to connect with anyone.

TOM wanders in with an almost empty PINT, checking his WATCH. He nods hello at CHLOE but doesn't approach.

CHLOE stirs COCKTAIL, feeling awkward.

TOM downs his PINT, placing it on TABLE near SCOREBOX.

In two minds, he regards his CARD, then drops it in SCOREBOX.

JOANNE enters, lugging a drunk JACQUI on her shoulder.

JOANNE

Make way, drunk girl coming through.

TOM

Oh! *That* Jacqui.

TOM rushes over to help.

JOANNE offloads JACQUI onto TOM's shoulder then rotates her stiff back.

CHLOE

Wow, she's wasted.

JACQUI

(Slurring) No I'm not!

JOANNE

Someone's been feeding her drinks.

JACQUI

Lemonades!

JOANNE

I'll try getting her home.

TOM

The organisers might have her address.

JOANNE

Are you okay with her?

TOM

As long as she doesn't hurk all over me.

JACQUI suddenly stands to point a finger at TOM.

JACQUI

Frankly, Scarlett Frankly, I don't give a shit.

TOM catches JACQUI as she falls back onto his shoulder.

TOM

Maybe hurry?

JOANNE rushes OFF.

TOM and CHLOE stand awkwardly, as JACQUI fades.

CHLOE

Remember me?

TOM

Sure. The no-shorties girl.

Dismayed by her lasting impression on him, CHLOE nods.

TOM

No jockeys tonight?

CHLOE

No jockeys. Though that was actually my friend.
Not me.

TOM

Friends can be like that, can't they.

CHLOE

Did you have a good night?

JACQUI burps in his ear.

TOM

Having the absolute night of my life. You?

CHLOE

Yeah. It was great.

TOM

Any matches?

CHLOE

Not really. You?

JACQUI clutches TOM like a teddy bear.

TOM

I wasn't really here to find anyone.

CHLOE nods, getting the message. She looks at her CARD.

CHLOE

Think I'll have a re-review in case I judged too harshly first-time round. Re-roll the dice.

TOM

I hope you find someone nice.

CHLOE

Go make me some serendipity. Unless my perfect match has been hiding in the toilets all night.

TOM

Is that likely?

CHLOE

No. That would be nuts.

CHLOE departs OFF, matching matching "faces" with names on her CARD.

JOANNE returns with her CARD.

JOANNE

A taxi is on the way.

TOM

Yay.

JACQUI

(Drunkenly joins in) Yayyyy!

JOANNE

I'll go with her to make sure she gets in safely.

JOANNE takes JACQUI from TOM, then totters her towards "DOOR".

TOM

Aren't you putting your card in?

JOANNE holds CARD in free hand.

JOANNE

That's where I wrote her address.

JOANNE guesses TOM's meaning.

JOANNE

Oh.

A moment of indecision for them. JACQUI's head lolls.

TOM steps forward then stops, almost surprised by his movement.

TOM

You'll need help getting her into the taxi.

JOANNE

Getting her out will be the real problem.

TOM

I could come along? To help.

JOANNE looks at her CARD.

JOANNE

Looks like we're headed North.

TOM

I live South.

JOANNE

Actually, I'm South too. We could … share a lift after?

JOANNE misinterprets TOM's hesitation.

JOANNE

No, you stay. Socialise.

TOM

Shit no, I've wanted to leave all night.

TOM rushes over to support JACQUI between them.

JOANNE

Don't you have friends here?

TOM

I do. And if we're *really* careful, we'll sneak right past them.

JACQUI blearily looks at him.

JACQUI

None of the above, buster!

JACQUI passes out again.

JOANNE

She is totally wasted.

TOM

To be honest, it's probably done her the world of good.

JOANNE and TOM lug JACQUI OFF.

CHLOE returns. She spots "someone", waves half-heartedly, forcing a smile.

CHLOE

Better one tick than none, Chloe.

She makes to mark her CARD but has no pen.

CHLOE

Shit. Pen, pen.

CHLOE pats pockets then looks for any pens lying around.

MIKE enters, immediately spotting CHLOE.

MIKE pauses decisively, then pops his collar to approach.

He stops and puts collar back down again.

CHLOE finally finds a PENCIL in her back pocket.

MIKE taps CHLOE's shoulder. She is surprised to see him.

MIKE

Hi.

CHLOE

Hi. ... Mark?

MIKE

Mike.

CHLOE

Oh. Sorry.

MIKE's momentum stalls.

CHLOE

We didn't actually meet tonight. Properly. During the rounds.

MIKE

No, we didn't.

MIKE offers her a PEN.

MIKE

Can I have your phone number?

CHLOE drops PENCIL in surprise.

LIGHTS down.

END

Principle Props

- Five TABLES and CHAIRS – one table must be sturdy enough to support a person standing on it.

- Score CARDS, PENCILS, PENS.

- Easily stuck/pinned NAMETAGs. Four of one colour, one different.

- mobile PHONES (two must be identical).

- PINT, WINE, WATER, and COCKTAIL glasses (with STRAWS).

- PHOTOGRAPHS.

- TOM and JACQUI have WATCHES.

- JACQUI has an extra NOTEPAD.

- TAROT CARDS.

- Cardboard BAR MATS.

- TOILET SIGN.

- BOWL OF NUTS/SNACKS.

- JACQUI has a HANDBAG with HAND SANITISER, MIRROR, LIPSTICK.

- JOANNE has a HANDBAG with a COMPACT.

- Handwritten, folded NOTE.

- An investment BROCHURE

- Drinks INVOICE.

- MIKE requires a number of increasingly sodden and stained SHIRTS.

- Large NUMBERED CARDS "5", "4", "3", "2", "1".

- Slotted, cheaply decorated cardboard box labelled "SCORE! BOX".

Glossary

- Pint glass – a common large drink size in Australian bars.

- Cosmo – a Cosmopolitan cocktail.

- "Dob me in" – tell on me/snitch.

- Rootin' (Rooting) – slang for sex.

- Scrags – derogatory insult for a drunk boyfriend-stealing girl of overly amenable disposition, usually from an equally drunk girl of scorned disposition.

- Ute – utility vehicle/SUV/truck/pick-up truck.

- Doof doof – slang for drum-heavy dance music.

- RSLs – social clubs where members of the Returned Soldiers League gather for drink prices and entertainment from the 1970's.

- Trackies – tracksuit pants.

- Hurk – slang meaning 'to vomit'.

- Ned Kelly – a historical bearded Australian bushranger (violent criminals who used the wilds to hide after committing crimes) famous for wearing metal armour plating and helmet, to mixed results.

- Cold Chisel – an Australian pub rock band from the 80's played incessantly on commercial radio, like *every* day. Seriously, *enough*, music programmers.

Interview with the Author

As part of a *Diary of a Play* series of blog posts, the author kindly recorded an interview with himself and a rather nice glass of wine for publicity purposes.

Q: So, "Spd D8n". How did that name come about? Random placement of Scrabble tiles?

A: You don't get a number eight tile in Scrabble.

Q: That's the last time I buy a board game cheap on eBay.

A: I figured the play couldn't be called "Speed Dating", or else you risked a whole bunch of people turning up expecting to find love via a strictly managed introduction format, instead getting a dodgy bit of independent theatre. And hey, *art*.

Q: Can audience members still expect to find love if they come along?

A: Hang about the bar after the show, theatre types are notoriously easy.

Q: Where did the idea for the play come from?

A: Ages ago, I blagged a free ticket to a speed dating night due to a dire shortage of guys. It sounded like a laugh, then the idea of just four minutes at a time to learn about a person struck me as an interesting concept for a play.

Q: Does this happen each time you go out somewhere?

A: Pretty much. Stay tuned for "I'm Just Popping Down to the Shops - the Musical".

Q: I don't think I will.

A: Fair enough. So, I went along, percolating this vague idea, then proceeded to have a whole bunch of odd conversations and encounters. From there, five characters began to take shape.

Q: Did you pick up?

A: Is that relevant? We're talking about the play.

Q: I think we can take that as a "No".

A: I started on my merry writing way, but eventually got stuck. Luckily, the same group was desperately short of guys again, so I blagged another free entry. And this time, some *really* odd stuff happened.

Q: Pick up?

A: Nup.

Q: *Dammmmmnn*, dude. Lift yo' game.

A: Combining these new encounters along with anecdotes from friends, and some blatant eavesdropping when my local pub hosted a few speed dating nights, the rest of the play worked itself out from there.

Q: And that's when you approached Blak Yak to put the show on.

A: Pretty much, yup.

Q: And then you faffed about on it for twelve odd months, continually promising them it was nearly ready.

A: Pretty much, yup.

Q: But now it's written?

A: Pretty much, yup.

Q: *Really* written?

A: I've recently taken a minor break, so as to have a fresh-eyed edit and tidy, along with any initial feedback from the director, and my own brutally critical opinion of everything that I write. Including letters to the milkman.

Q: But it is *actually* written? I'm not asking for myself, but for certain theatre committee members who have just booked a theatre and started publicising it.

A: It's really very nearly ready.

Q: Are you lying?

A: ... no.

Interview ended, after a long doubtful stare between both parties.

About the Author

Martin Lindsay is a Western Australian writer hidden away in the leafy seaside town of Dunsborough.

He is the author of the plays *Spd D8n*, *One Night One Day* and *Brown Acid*, and award-winning one-act plays *One Night Stand Off* and *Past Loves*.

Other plays include one-act *Someone Called Rob*, and finalists in the Short + Sweet and Arkfest ten-minute play festivals with *Couch*, *The Retirement Gift*, *That Little Voice*, and *Possum Play*.

Martin was a contributing writer for *Lifted* in the 2013 Perth Fringe Festival, and co-wrote and directed the comedy monologue/burlesque *Lock-In Love* for the 2014 Adelaide Fringe Festival and 2014 Melbourne Comedy Festival.

Martin's short stories have been included in Black Inc's *Best Australian Stories 2012*, and won the 2013 Stringybark Humorous Short Story Competition, the 2014 Joe O'Sullivan Writers Prize, and the 2019 Peter Cowan Short Story award. His micro-fiction has appeared in Short and Twisted editions and Night Parrot Press' *Once* (2020), *Twice Not Shy* (2021), and *Three Can Keep a Secret* (2022) collections.

He is even known to occasionally blog on his website at martinlindsay.net, when not trying to stop parrots from having sex on his balcony railing.

Martin's debut novel *Wil, Maree and the Mattress* will be available soon from Moody Lapcat Books.

Plays by the Same Author

- One Night One Day

- Brown Acid

- Someone Called Rob

- Past Loves

- Couch

- Framed

- The Retirement Gift

- That Little Voice

- Possum Play

- Third Date's the Charm

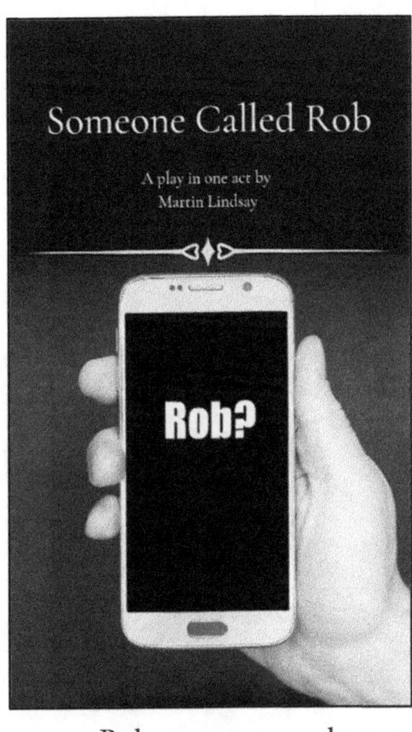

Someone Called Rob

A play in one act by Martin Lindsay

Sometimes it pays to just let the call go through to voicemail...

Rob answers an unknown caller on his mobile.

An angry guy called Adam reveals just what Rob did last night. That's why Adam is angry.

And *everyone* knows what happens when Adam gets angry.

And Adam has Rob's phone number...

As Rob learns, a lot can be discovered from just a phone number.

Available now from Moody Lapcat Books.

Past Loves

A play in one act by Martin Lindsay

Ben is having a very good year. It just doesn't happen to be the current one.

Invited to coffee by his best mate's wife, Ben's life … lives … are about to be turned upside down.

And not just by the price of a latte these days.

'It *happened before I could stop it. If I'd only known where things would go …'*

'*Where did things go?'*

'*Where do you think things went!'*

'*I've heard a lot about <u>you</u>, Ben.'*

'*This will work much better with open minds.'*

'*If not completely vacant ones.'*

Available now from Moody Lapcat Books.

One Night
One Day

**A play in two acts by
Martin Lindsay**

A comedy about singles and social graces, after a night that went so right goes so wrong the next morning.

Rachel and Greg wake up together after a night out on the town, much to the surprise of both.

An awkward situation at the best of times, made all the more awkward as details from the previous night slowly filter back to them…

Coming soon from Moody Lapcat Books.

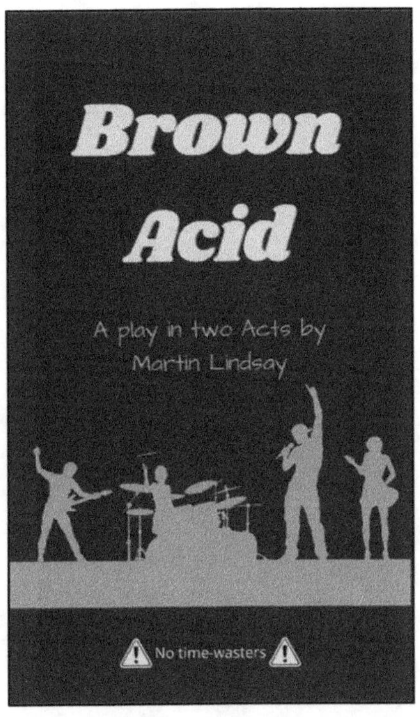

Brown Acid

**A play in two acts by
Martin Lindsay**

Throughout rock'n'roll
history, from small
beginnings sometimes
legendary bands grow ...

And sometimes, they
don't.

Wanted:

Musicians to join original four-piece rock band.

Serious gigging opportunities with a group that is going
places. Own transport would suit.

NO TIME WASTERS!

Coming soon from Moody Lapcat Books.

Moody Lapcat Books

Books better than belly rubs

Moody Lapcat Books is an independent publisher of books and plays.

Visit <u>moodylapcatbooks.com</u> to see our latest releases, things to come, or enquire about performance rights.

Or <u>contact@moodylapcatbooks.com</u>